Tale of a Mafia Princess

Published by IAMWORDS Press
Copyright © 2011 by MaDonna Akua

ISBN −0983445540

ISBN −9780983445548

First Printing April 2012

Edited By: Valonda Harris, Christie Gardner

Printed in the United States of America

2011942280

Contact Sankofa - @Sankofarose - Twitter

www.facebook.com/sankofawrites - Facebook

Acknowledgements

In a million years I never thought I would be penning the acknowledgements for my SECOND novel! My dreams have surely come true and this is only the tip of the iceberg. I am eternally grateful to the best graphic designer in the world Junnita Jackson, to every person who purchased Devyne Envy and all the short stories I have online, to the numerous book clubs who have shown me so much love, all of the social media love, the ALL4ONE group on Facebook, everyone who pushed my book helped me promote (Alisha my manager/bff Chadd Scott/my other manager) Team Seven1Seven Soul who always makes sure they are big upping and supporting my passion, and last but not least my 2 amigos TEAM #IAMWORDS. These two, Cm Spence and Tiger Rose push me to go hard and be a better me, to keep going when I want to quit and to strive for excellence in everything I produce. When I win, we all win.

Sankofa

For every woman who was ever a daddy's girl.

Preface

The cross hanging behind the pulpit felt as if it was strapped to my back as I slowly walked to my seat in the church. The scent of roses was thick in the air. There were so many people, I felt so out of place. "*Oh my goodness*," I thought, as the hairs rose on the nape of my neck, I could feel all eyes on me. Whispers rose like a soft breeze from every corner of the sanctuary:

"There she is."

"How dare she show her face in here!"

My soul hurt and my heart lay heavy in the pit of my stomach. I tried to take my seat as the choir sang. Today I bury my boyfriend Jordan, whose life was taken at the hands of my father.I am Londyn and this is my story.

3 months later

Chapter 1

Londyn

My lips pulsed quickly around the tip of his penis as his glimmering white 750Li rolled to a stop right before my front door. I popped it out of my mouth and smiled as I admired the ring of Ruby Woo lipstick I'd left at the base of his shaft.

"Your wife and I should have a lipstick party. To see who can swallow more of your dick."

"If only I could be so lucky." Javier closed his eyes surely dreaming of a ménage trois.

"Whatever. Call me later- or not." I adjusted my bra and tank top and hopped out of the car then went into the house. Walking through the door I was greeted by a familiar voice.

"Your father would like to see you Ms. Londyn," Thomas, our family's long standing butler, said as I walked through the door.

"So what else is new?" It irritated my soul to no end the way my heels clicked against the hand-laid marble floor. The sound was worse than nails on a chalk board. I removed my shoes and sauntered past the oversized table in the foyer. Ivan and Sergio, my father's resident snitches, stood on either side of his huge oak office door.

"Excuse me fellows,I was summoned by your leader." I pushed past them into my father's office.

"Ay, watch it Londyn!"

"Kiss my ass." I pinned my hair up and pulled down my super short electric blue mini skirt. I slowly made my way over to the desk where my father, Giuseppe Taliaferro, was seated. His office, lined with picture windows made it hard not to marvel at the sweeping landscapes and rolling hills just beyond each window pane.

"Who dropped you in front of the door?" My father's tone was even, steady, cold and calculating. There is rarely a moment when you would find him saying things he doesn't mean. "Sergio informed me there was a white 750Li in the driveway."

"Daddy, I don't owe you any explanations, who and what I do is my business."

"Londyn you belong to me!" my Daddy yelled.

"I belonged to Jordan but you killed any chance of that happening!" I took a seat in one of the huge leather chairs that stood in front of his desk. This stupid desk was one of my father's prized possessions; he cared for it like it was a baby, having it polished and primed often, just because it was once owned by Al Capone.

"Daddy, I'm sure you have more pressing matters to attend to, like who to off next!"

"Watch your tone with me young lady, you have forgotten who you are talking to." The veins in my father's neck began to raise and pulsate.

"Oh excuse me, Don Taliaferro! Don Murderer is more like it." I mumbled under my breath and rolled my eyes.

3

"I have enrolled you into college. You start St. Joseph's in two weeks. You have an appointment with the Dean of Students at 9 am tomorrow morning."

"Why in the hell do I need to go to school? Aren't we rich?"

"Education is important Mi Bella Dona. That's my final word."

"Whatever,Daddy!" I stormed out of his office through the foyer to the kitchen, almost knocking over Rosie, our maid. She was feeding our family dog, Nicodemus.

"Sorry Rosie, I didn't see you!"

"No worries Ms. Londyn, would you like something to snack on before dinner?"

"No, I'm good thank you." I stuck my head in the fridge then ducked out of the back door and ran across the lawn to the guest house; my palace.

"Who in the hell does he think he is? Trying to make me go to school? I am not the daughter of one of his lawyer friends! I am the daughter of a king, that makes me a princess and I shouldn't have to do shit!" I stripped my clothes off and drew myself a bath in my jacuzzi. *"You are one sexy bitch Londyn,"* I thought to myself as I grabbed my vibrator and searched for the warm spot in between my legs to pleasure myself. *"Later for this school shit."*

***

The next morning the registration office was filled with current and would be students. I had to make it quick in this place because I had a hot date. *"I am determined to fuck every man in the world if it will piss off my daddy."* I donned my best Cavalli dress with no panties. My black Stuart Weitzman sky walkers made my ass sit up higher than usual. I make it my business to look like a million dollars every fucking day.

"Good Morning, how can I help you," the little receptionist squeaked from behind her desk.

"I have an appointment with the dean or something." The little lady made a call and then led me through a glass door to the dean's office. I took a seat and waited to be called. *"I can't believe Giuseppe's on this bull shit."*

The dean's office was stuffy, as if sunlight never reached beyond its walls.

"Good Morning Ms. Taliaferro. So, are you excited about becoming a student here at St. Joseph's University?" The dean was a sexy older man, olive skin like my father but with salt and pepper hair.

"Dean Jones, can I call you Donald?" I said crossing and uncrossing my legs in front of him so he could get a glimpse of my freshly shaved snatch.

"Dean Jones or Dr. Jones will do just fine Ms. Taliaferro."

"Please, call me Londyn."

"Ok…Londyn." I could see him adjusting himself in his seat. The platinum band on his ring finger sealed the deal. He was mine for the taking. I stood up and leaned across his desk. My perky double D breasts danced before his eyes.

"What I need to know is what a young, sexy intelligent woman like myself needs to do to get on the dean's list?" I climbed across his desk and placed one leg on either side of his chair. My twat was fully exposed to him now and he dove in to it like he hadn't seen or tasted a pussy like mine in ages.

"I'm cumming, I'm cumming! Don't stop!" I said as I pushed my hips forward and his tongue danced around on my clit. I tore his tie from his neck and stuffed it in my mouth to stifle my moans.

"You like this?" Dean Jones said to me as he took his pudgy sausage fingers and stuffed them into my pussy hole.

"Are you going to keep doing me like this baby?"

"Just keep that fresh pussy coming my way and you won't have to do a damn thing."

"And you can have all of my daddy's money that he's paying for this place." I slid down off of his desk, grabbed a tissue to wipe the wetness from legs, and I strutted out of his office, pulling my skirt down.

Paulette

I hoped to surprise Donald with a lunch date. He'd been so busy lately, we rarely had time to do anything. I must have checked myself in the mirror a thousand times, making sure my shirt was properly covering my tire sized midsection. I ran my fingers through my strawberry blonde hair as I walked off the elevator and into the lobby. The most beautiful woman I had ever seen was shutting the door to my husband's office as I was coming through the reception area. She was the prettiest color tan, her skinned glowed, it reminded me of one of the Brazilian girls that you see on television. I cut my eyes at her as she walked towards the elevator. Her smell was captivating, unlike anything that pierced my olfactory senses before.

"Who was that woman leaving my husband's office, Diane? I THOUGHT you said he wasn't in? What is that she's wearing?"

"Mrs. Jones I apologize I could have sworn I saw him leave. His appointment with Ms. Taliaferro was supposed to end 40 minutes ago. I think that was a mirage. I'm not sure I could be wrong." Diane was a mousey introverted woman; she's been my husband's receptionist for the past 15 years. She'd be better suited as a librarian.

"Taliaferro? As in Giuseppe Taliaferro?"

"Yes, I believe so. Her name is Londyn." Diane shuffled her papers and never looked up from her computer screen.

"I have a bad feeling about her. I bet my life that little bitch is no student."I knocked on the door and Donald's loving smiled greeted me.

"Hello dear. I just got done with enrollment counseling. What are you doing here?" He was a bit flush and his tie was sloppily re-tied.

"Since when are you in charge of enrollments? Isn't that Eric's job? Or Katie?" I studied his face for a sign that he was lying to me.

"Darling, I'm hungry, let's grab a bite to eat, it was no big deal, overflow work and I wanted to do my part." He grabbed me by the hand and pulled me to him. He smelled sweaty. My intuition was telling me something was going on. *"I'm going to find out exactly what it is."*

Giuseppe

Behind the pristine white walls of Taliaferro and Associates I was seen as a God and my boardroom was where I sent men to heaven or damned them to hell.

"Mr. Taliaferro, Demetrius Aramoso is requesting you on first chair at his trial."

"We have mutual friends; please advise him that I will be there."

"Not a problem, sir." My newest paralegal said, making a note of it in his day planner.

"Give me the details of the case fellas." I leaned back in my chair and let my associates give me the run down.

Londyn

Stepping off the elevator I fixed my dress a bit and removed my Chanel sunglasses. I walked up to the front desk where a little blonde bitch was sitting pretending to be interested in her work. My fresh tan made my copper colored skin glow and I was sure this pasty faced bitch was jealous. I rolled my eyes.

"Can you tell him I'm here?"

"I'm sorry, who would you like to see?" Pasty Face said, while smacking her gum.

"OKAY, since you are obviously new here, I'll give you the benefit of the doubt. I need to see my father, Mr. Taliaferro."

I walked past her before she could tell me he was unavailable. With my registration papers in hand, I headed down the hallway straight for his office. His door was open but the office was empty. I switched my tight ass down the hallway to the boardroom. *"He has to be in here."* I stuck my head in as he was signing briefs and listening to his yes men. *'The work of a mob boss/lawyer is never done.'*

"Can I speak to you?" I asked, irritated that I had to even show my face. My father stood up and excused himself from the boardroom briefly.
His walk was stately and the tailoring on his Armani suit was impeccable. *"He had to be the most handsome Italian man I had ever seen."* Most Dons were out of shape, old and unattractive. My father is only 42 and with all the style and charm of the old world he is a force to be reckoned with.

"Mia Bella Dona, what have I told you about wearing these kinds of clothes? When did all this start?" My father said as he grabbed me tightly by my arm and walked me down the hallway.

"I just came to show you the proof that I went to that appointment. If you don't like my clothes then buy me something else!" I tried to loosen my father's grip to no avail.

"Give me those papers. Take my black card, spend no more than a thousand, Bella, don't fuck with me. If I see one unauthorized purchase, I will rip every item you own to shreds myself."
A tear started to well up in the corner of my eye. I quickly regained my composure and the fire that was ignited in my father's eyes was gone. It was replaced by the loving eyes I have looked upon since I was born.

"Thank you daddy, I'll see you at home." I slid his card into my Vuitton purse and skipped down the hallway towards to lobby. As I passed by the water

9

cooler I winked and licked my lips in the direction of a sexy guy who was filling his water bottle.

Giuseppe

My newest employee joined me in stride back to the board room.

"Hey, Mr. T, that's a tight little piece of moulie ass ya got there. I'd love to bend that over!"

My eyes glazed over. As my naïve employee took his seat I grabbed a letter opener from the drawer. I stood behind this fuck face who thought his blatant disrespect was funny. He obviously didn't know me. His laughter was replaced by sheer terror as I leaned his head back and placed the letter opener to his neck.

"If you ever speak of my daughter in that manner again, I will draw more than just a trickle of blood from your throat." I threatened as

crimson droplets stained the collar of his fresh white dress shirt and the little bastard passed out.

Chapter 2

Londyn

"Fuck I need to figure out what to wear!" I complained to my best friend Corynne as I tossed aside one designer item after the next.

"Uhh, didn't your dad just give you money to shop with earlier?" Corynne walked through my closet and ogled at my vast collection of shoes, dresses and purses. Corynne's father is a US Diplomat from the Dominican Republic and her mother was one of the first black runway models.

"So tell me about this date you have tonight Lon, who is he?"

"He's the dean of the school daddy enrolled me in, trying to get me to get an education. That's who I need to fuck to get where I need to be."

"Fucking and sucking to get over Jordan is not going to make the pain go away." Corynne tried to place her hand on my shoulder as I sank into my chaise lounge. She was pretty ditsy for the most part but every once in a while she would share some really poignant words.

"Jordan loved me for me, for who I was. Not because I was rich or connected, but for me!" I turned away from Corynne as I spilled my soul onto the floor of my dressing room..

"It's bad enough that my mother was so afraid of my father's family that she abandoned me and ran away… because, because," tears welled up in my eyes even though I tried to hold them back. I shut my eyes tightly as the pain I was feeling rushed from my chest and formed my words. "Because she was black…she wasn't good enough to marry my father, she never stood up to them, she just ran. Jordan stood up to my father and made his intentions known and now he's gone!" Corynne stood in shock; I rarely had emotional breakdowns. My father's motto was"Never let 'em see you cry."

"Lon, girl, maybe you should see somebody. You know my mom has like two therapists on speed dial!" I dried my tears and stood to my feet. The plush carpeting massaged my perfectly manicured toes.

"Bitch you're crazy and I have a date! Let's see if I can fuck my way to Valedick-torian!

Paulette

So I Googled that little bitch only to find out that she is the Paris Hilton of Philadelphia, the daughter of the most prominent criminal attorney in the tri-state area, Giuseppe Taliaferro. I read on, unable to turn away from the screen: "It is suspected that Taliaferro's ties go deeper than just representation of these Mafioso," according to the gossip sites. "So they call you the mafia princess.there's something not quite right about you, little Ms. Londyn." I quickly shut my laptop and resumed my television watching. Donald came down stairs and grabbed his jacket from the hall closet.

"Paulette, I am stepping out. I will return shortly."

"Donald, the lecture series you have been wanting to see for several weeks is on in 30 minutes!" Donald continued towards the door without looking up.

"DVR it for me dear, and don't wait up."
As he closed the door and stepped out into the brisk summer air, I reopened my laptop. The search was on for a private detective.

Giuseppe

"I have called this meeting of the four families because we have an unresolved issue. I am disturbed by the death of my daughter's boyfriend,Jordan Walters." My favorite restaurant Si'Sicily was owned by Don Carmelengo; a close personal friend. Meetings about family business were always held over dinner.

"Giuseppe, I have consulted my associates, we know nothing about this unfortunate incident." Don Aridano said as he stuffed his face with fresh cannoli. The restaurant was very old world, which felt so much like home. Italian music and
love is spread to all who enter.

"I need to find out who did this one. They put my signature on it." I lit my cigar and let the Cuban aroma fill my lungs and cloud my mind. The sun waved good bye from the banks of the Jersey shore and nightfall set in.

"Giuseppe it will be my honor to put my best men on it." Don Scoda was a long time confidant of mine.
When my father was killed and his body was thrown from the top of a high rise, it was Don Scoda's decision to grant me power over my organization at just 30 years old. I had just entered into my law practice and thus the perfect cover job was born. A Don with a clean jacket is unheard of, until now.

"This hit a little close to home my friends. Someone will answer for this blatant disrespect." I rose from the table and looked into the faces of each of the men before me, trying to read the truth in
one of their eyes.

"Salutare." They simultaneously raised their glasses and replied.

"Si, salutare."

Londyn

The sounds of Beyonce's "Party" had me bopping my head to the beat as my Maserati hugged the curves on the expressway. I hadn't spoken to Jordan's mom, Ms. Latrice, in the three months since the funeral. I wanted to stop by and bring her a card and some flowers, just to see how she was doing. I slowed and looked for parking on the tiny, dimly lit Newkirk Street.

Jordan's neighborhood was so bad. I often got nervous when I went alone, but not when I was with him. He would sit me out on the block with him and I would feel so safe. The girls from my school, even Corynne, would swear I was slumming but in all reality he was too good for me.

He was comfortable being who he was; I'm the one who always had to put on a show. I walked up the four steps to Jordan's mother's door. There was a crowd of girls outside of the house and I recognized one of them as Jordan's cousin, Honor. In front of the abandoned house next door there stood a makeshift memorial. Candles flickered and lit up the collage of my baby, making him look like an angel.

"Saint Jordan, my angel," I said to myself as I rang his mother's door bell.

"I know this bold, high yellow bitch ain't show her face ova this way!" Honor stepped over in front of Jordan's house and blocked the steps.

"I can go anywhere I please! Jordan was MY man!" I rang the doorbell again, then stuck the flowers and card in the screen door.

"Bitch, he wasn't your man, he was your way to seem as if you were down. You're nothing but a half breed whore! Because of your smut ass my cousin is dead!" Honor continued to block me from stepping down off the steps. The pain in her eyes matched mine. I stepped down off the step and my eyes met with hers.

"Look, Honor, let me explain something to you. Jordan was my everything; I loved him so much, I can't take back what happened. I have his name tattooed on my chest, he is eternally in my heart. What the fuck else do you want me to do?" I pushed past her and shoulder bumped the girl directly next to her. Honor pushed me and I faltered. My hands went out in front of me and I fell. A swarm of girls formed around me and I couldn't see where I was going.

"Get the fuck away from me!" I screamed.

"Bitch, you got J-Styles killed, I should kill you!" One girl with micro braids and glasses said as she pulled my hair.

"I'm a rip all your fucking hair out, you bougie-ass bitch. You got some fucking nerve." Honor drew spit from the base of her throat and spat into my face. I could hear a man's voice from overhead.

"Back the fuck up off her! Now y'all!" The crowd parted and Jordan's brother Darrius made his way towards me. He extended his hand to me and helped me up off the ground.

"Y'all act like y'all don't know who she is, keep fucking with her. You will end up in body bags too!" Darrius's eyes were cold as he helped me to my car.

"Thank you so much, brother," I said as I started up my ride.

"Don't get it twisted; I'm not your brother. I don't fuck with you either. I just ain't trying to have no more family going to the morgue."

Paulette

As I stood before the fire place in my spacious living room I glanced at my watch, 4:05 am. My mind reeled. I looked in the mirror and examined myself in the light; with each step I took my extra weight reminded me how unattractive I truly was. I heard the rumble and purr of my husband's Porsche as it pulled into the driveway. My heart stood still as
he turned his key in the door.

"I told you not to wait up."

"I didn't wait up. I just woke up to get something to settle my stomach," I lied. I couldn't sleep thinking he was out somewhere having a roll in the hay with that little bitch.

Donald was in an exceptionally good mood. I followed him up the steps and took a seat on the edge of our bed. "Donald what is that on you? Perfume?"He sat up, irritated that I was calling him on the one thing that was so obvious.

"Woman, what are you rambling about?"
I pulled on his shirt and twisted the hair on the back of his head in between my fingers.

"When is the last time you had an orgasm?"
"Paulette, you don't fuck me so I wouldn't know."

Chapter 3

Giuseppe

The rain fell from the sky in buckets as my driver slowed to a stop in front of the federal court house.

"Here you are Mr. Taliaferro, sir." He held the umbrella for me as I exited my Maybach and stepped out onto the curb.

"Good luck in court today sir."

"Why thank you Lucas. I'll do what I can. This seems like a tough one!" I winked at him as he returned to his side of the car. I entered through the massive stone doors to the security station, placed my brief case on conveyer belt and stepped through the metal detector.

"Morning Mr. Taliaferro," a tall Russian fellow greeted me as I collected my things and moved towards the lobby. Handshakes and hellos are never few and far between when I set foot in a courtroom. The main thoroughfare of the court house was packed with men and women shackled at their wrists and ankles; an endless sea of Department of Corrections uniforms stretched the length of the hallway. "Great it's court week," I muttered as I turned down the hallway to courtroom C. On either side of the entrance to the court room the scales of justice loomed accusingly overhead.

Demetrius Aramoso is what I can describe as a world class fuck up. His father was first lieutenant in the Scoda crime family, which allowed Demetrius to rank in the family via legacy. He's what I would call 10 short of a dozen all day long. In the heat of the moment this numb nuts catches his girlfriend sucking off some dope dealer. She was high as a kite off smack. So not only does he beat the dog shit out of her he shoots the guy and burns down the hotel. *"I'm supposed to defend this loose cannon? Come on! Now one thing I will say is that his father is a genius when it comes to finding ways out of sticky situations. Let's see what he comes up with."*
Closed court proceedings make for much less drama. They are a favorite of mine. Demetrius sat smugly in his chair as I made my way to the table and sat down beside him.

"Mornin' Mr. Taliaferro, my fatha sends his love and appreciation for what ya doin fa us here." Demetrius was a little man with a Napoleon complex. Standing all of 5'5", he over compensated for his vertical challenges by driving the best and wearing the best. Above all things, he's stupid as hell, so he often gets his ass handed to him.

"Good Morning, now briefly explain to me what the fuck is going on."

"There's nothing to explain Mr. T, I'm innocent!"

"Yea okay, and I'm Jewish. Just keep your mouth shut till I say otherwise." The jury filed into the courtroom and a hush fell over everyone.

"All rise, the honorable Judge Margaret Cragwell presiding," The bailiff boomed across the room.

"You may be seated. What do we have here? The Commonwealth of Pennsylvania VS. Demetrius Aramoso? Ah, Mr. Aramoso so lovely to see you again. We still haven't learned our lesson I see." Judge Cragwell surveyed the courtroom and locked eyes with my client.

"Ay ya judgeship, I just came to see you! I have nothing to do with these trumped up accusations," Demetrius put on his best innocent face but the judge's eyes remained cold.

"Mr. Taliaferro, please proceed with opening statements." Judge Cragwell shuffled papers and looked over at Assistant District Attorney Cheryl Wright who was smiling as if the case was already won for her.

I rose from my seat and crossed the court room, pausing for a moment before I spoke.

"When the prosecutor read the indictment I saw the look of horror on your faces. This is a despicable crime. What could be more horrible than being beaten to a pulp then burned alive? I just want you to know that this man," I said as I walked over to Demetrius and placed my hand on his shoulder, "This man, Demetrius Aramoso did not commit this crime. Mr. Aramoso is not guilty. That, esteemed men and women of the jury, brings us to what Judge Cragwell has given us 20 minutes to talk about – getting blamed for something you didn't do." I turned to take my seat and locked eyes with a little old woman in the jury box who winked at me.

When the one and only witness got up to take the stand Demetrius began to fidget in his seat. I patted him on his back and leaned over towards him.

"Don't get nervous. I'm going to get her on cross examination." He nodded his head in unwilling agreement. The witness was Star Rodriguez, an infamous local prostitute and female pimp. She was not a day over 26, but looked well over 40 from all of the abuse and mistreatment to her body. Her waist length hair flowed in the air conditioned breeze. Her hips moved hypnotically as she stepped up to the witness stand.

"Please state your name for the court."

Smacking her gum loudly she replied, "Star Lynn Rodriguez."

I was not prepared for what happened next. As Star was being sworn into testimony the little old lady in the jury box stood up and removed a plastic gun from the sleeve of her sweater.

"Shhhee's got a gun!" A person in the jury box cried out. Three shots sailed rapidly across the courtroom and pierced Star's chest.

"¡Dios mío!" Star cried as she crumpled into the chair in the witness stand. Before the bailiffs could make it over to the older woman in the jury box she screamed,

"Morte Alla Francia Italia Anelia[1]." She then turned the gun on herself and fell lifelessly onto the man seated next to her.

Paulette

It tears my nerves how Donald would rather screw this little whore than me. I know I am far from the spring chicken I used to be, however I am nowhere near chopped liver. I sipped my Diet Pepsi and scoured the internet until I found a detective worth his salt. My third eye is telling me Donald is fucking around.

"Newsflash to the bloodsucking cunts who want my husband; he belongs to me!"

Darowich and Son was the third agency I contacted; most just located deadbeat dads for prosecution of child support. I crossed my tubby pale legs and contemplated hiring a male escort to take me to unknown levels of ecstasy.

"Fuck it, after I get Donald for everything he's worth I'll find myself a bare chested Mexican in dire need of a green card." The sun shone through the window of my study and refracted off the crystal

---

[1] *The Anagram for the word MAFIA.*

hanging just above my desk. It normally made my morning to see my private space engulfed in rainbows and light. However today I was in no mood. I chewed anxiously on the cap of my pen as I waited to be transferred to an investigator.

"I can't believe you Donald; you're willing to throw away 20 years of marriage over a mid-life crisis and a rich whore? My God just buy a new sports car and get over it," I thought to myself as I waited on hold. The line clicked and the voice of what sounded like an overweight middle aged man came across the line.

"Ted Darowich, What can I do ya for?" He chuckled. He obviously found himself amusing. I pulled the phone away from my ear as Ted let out a deep bronchial cough. *"He probably smokes,"* I thought.

"Hello, good morning sir. I am in need of your services."

"Well whadda ya need? Ya need background checks? Investigations? Lemme know."

"I'm looking for the latter."

"A ladder? Lady this ain't no tool shop, this is a professional establishment." A bit of irritation formed in his voice.

"Oh, I'm sorry Mr. Darowich maybe you misunderstood me."

"Please lil' lady call me Ted."

"Well Ted, I need to investigate my husband. I believe he's being unfaithful."

"That's not good, now is it?"

"No sir, and it troubles me greatly."

"Shit, I'd be downright pissed off! Ok so who is the bastard? Give me some details."

"My husband's name is Dr. Donald Jones."

"See it's these medical fucks who ruin it for the rest of us working stiffs."

"He's not a medical doctor he's a doctor of education."

"Yea, yea, yea, same thing. So lookey here, it's $400.00 a day. I do my thing. Bada bing, bada boom you got proof he's banging the maid."

"Ok, that will be fine. Only thing it's not my maid. It's Londyn Taliaferro." The words escaped my lips before I had a chance to stop them.

"Holy horse shit!" It sounded as if he sat straight up in his chair.

"Ya husband's doing the mafia princess? Fuck outta here!"

My heart raced. *"What if he won't take the case,"* I thought as I rose to my feet and walked towards the kitchen. *"Food will make me feel better."*

"Yes Ted that's who I believe he's having the affair with. Will that be a problem?" I grabbed the mayo and mustard from the refrigerator door and set them on the counter. Mr. Zonkers, my aging Himalayan cat, brushed up against my leg wanting to join in my morning gluttony.

"Not a problem ma'am we will get the job done. Not to worry. I will be in touch." I hung up the phone, straddled the stool in my kitchen, and fed my discontent.

Chapter 4

Londyn

I was checking my flawless make-up in my Dior compact as our driver for the evening pulled up to the 40/40 club in Atlantic City. It's rare I ever get carded, I'm a star. It was always packed Thursday through Sunday. The line was wrapped around the complex but waiting is not something we ever had to do.

"The freaks come out at night!" I screamed as we climbed the steps to the entrance. Corynne had on a KLS collection dress straight off the runway in Paris. Often mistaken for Eva Marchand; Corynne was fly. Darker than me, like almost a deep caramel, with a short firecracker bronze haircut. Her crowning achievement was a row of tribal symbols, called "adinkra" or something, etched from behind her left ear down to her wrist. Her Dominican heritage really shone through in her figure. It was phenomenal.

"Girl, yes all the freaks are out and waiting in line," Corynne said to me as we got to the top of the stairs at the club.

"What's up Londyn? Corynne? How are my two favorite party goers," said the club's promoter and event specialist, Tyree.

He was always good for pointing out the down low brothers in the club. He could often be heard saying, "Unh uh girl, I wouldn't do that one if I was you!"

"Hey Ty, what's up?" I kissed him on his cheek as he led us inside. I handed Tyree my credit card. "Charge it up boo!"

"I need a few good drinks and a good dance partner," Corynne yelled over the music .She scanned the crowd as we made our way to VIP.

"Now ladies you will be sharing VIP with Andre Igoudalla and some other 76er's, is that cool?" Tyree snapped a VIP bracelet on each of our arms.

"I want next to that tall, ball-playing piece of chocolate!"

"Cory you're crazy as hell. I swear you'll fuck anyone be it man or woman."

"I'm a get it where I can get it! That's my motto!"

"Whatever girl, that man is not even cute!

"Oh, but he is! Anything over 6'2" can have me anyway they want me!"

The club grooved and bumped heavy with bass as we settled into our lounge chairs.

"I'll have a Georgia Peach. She will have a Whore on Wheels," I said to the chesty waitress as she jotted down my order and ran to the bar to retrieve it. Chesty girl was quick with our order. I closed my eyes as I sipped my drink from the straw. letting the warmth of the alcohol soothe my chest. I downed two more drinks and I was hype; ready to dance the night away.

"Come on Cory," I said grabbing Corynne's hand and dragging her to her feet.

"I was just about to get his number Lon!" Corynne whined.

"Uh...like you were even close! Come on this is my song!" We entered the dance floor just as Eve's "Tambourine" was being mixed with Busta's "Make It Clap". I swirled my hips to the beat and bounced my ass better than the prize act at the strip joint. I felt a pair of hands groping my sides. I leaned into the grip because it felt familiar.

"Hello my love." It was Kelvin the married NFL cornerback who begged to suck my pussy on a regular basis. He was 6'3 and chocolate as hell. Just like I like my men; good enough to eat!

"Hey sexy I've missed you. You must be playing husband this month." I rubbed my ass on the bulge growing in his pants. I got wet just imagining his head between my legs.

"I've been busy baby. You drunk already?" he said to me as he helped me maintain my balance. "You and Corynne dancing y'all asses off, you're covered in sweat!" Kelvin rubbed his hands across the sweat mark that had formed in the back of my dress. A drop of sweat stung my eye. I wiped my brow and twisted my hair up into a bun.

"It's fucking hot in here I should take this off." I pulled my dress off over my head. I continued to dance to the beat, completely oblivious to the paparazzi in the crowd snapping picture after picture of me in my bra and panties.

29

The sun leaked through my blinds in streams piercing my eyelids, begging me to rise and meet the day. I slid on my Juicy Couture sweatpants and matching jacket. Quickly grabbing my cellphone, I jogged across the yard to the main house for breakfast.

"Hey Nicodemus! That's a good boy." I rubbed his furry head. He barked loudly at my entrance into the kitchen. Breakfast was always served in the dining room. I don't think I've ever seen a more beautiful room in all the places I've ever been. The walls are the faintest color yellow and aged to look like Italian stone. On the ceiling my father had a replica of the mural from the Sistine chapel painted. Every detail was exact. When I was little I use to lay on the floor and stare at it for hours. My father would ask me what I was doing and I would say I was talking to God.

"Good Morning Daddy," I said kissing him on top of his head and taking my seat next to him at the table for breakfast.

"Morning, Mia Bella Dona. Did you and Corynne have fun last night?"

"It was ok, you know girls night out," I said taking a sip of the orange juice Rosie set before me.

"40/40 hunh? Where's that over there next to Trump Plaza?"

"Daddy I didn't go to the 40/40 last night. What made you think that?"

"What made me think that? Page fucking six of the daily news that's what!" My father slammed down the newspaper. His coffee spilled over and splashed all over me.

"Naked in a night club? Come on be for real!"
I grabbed a napkin to blot off the coffee that was quickly staining my sweatsuit.

"Daddy I'm growing tired of these arguments, aren't you?" The tone in my voice was condescending as hell. My father hated it. I loved it. *"I don't care if I embarrass or disgrace my family,"* I thought to myself.

"I wasn't naked, as you can clearly see I had on a bra and panty set." My father's wrath was not to be taken lightly. I knew when to push buttons and when to back off.

"Londyn I am ordering you never to embarrass me like that again." My father walked away from the table just as Rosie was serving breakfast. "Rosie I've lost my appetite, thank you anyway." Turning away from the window that seemed to have him hypnotized my father looked at me with so much pain in his eyes.

"Bella what in the hell is going on with you? I'll go crazy trying to figure you out." He threw his hands up.

I smirked and my father walked out of the room. Chuckling I grabbed the newspaper. I'm a little vain. I wanted to see what they wrote about me. The caption under the picture read, "Lusty Londyn, always a play toy, never a bride." It pained me a bit but fuck it. I've been called worse by more important people. I almost choked on my bagel when I turned the page. Big as day was the heading, "Sherriff's Sale". When I saw the first address on the list my heart sank. *"244 Newkirk Street. Oh my God that's Jordan's mom's house!"*

***

My bleach white 7 jeans and RPD tank was the perfect attire to go pick up my books from the campus library- or so I thought. I picked up Corynne who was clearly hung over from the night before.

"Where are we going because my head is on blast," Corynne said sliding into the passenger seat of my freshly washed Maserati.

"I have to go to that school to pick up something. Then we can grab a bite at Chipotle in a few." I merged into the left lane and was almost cut off by a blue Honda.

"Fucker!" I yelled out the window. "If Jordan was here he'd kick that guy's ass." I let out a nervous laugh and looked over at Corynne who had the strangest look of empathy on her face. When we pulled up to the campus bookstore Corynne let out a tiresome groan.

"A library? What the fuck Lon?"

"It's not a library, blondie, it's a bookstore! I have to pick up my class materials," I said to her as we walked through the revolving door.

"Blondie? Huh, look at the pot calling the kettle! And libraries and bookstores are the same thing. They both have books! Duh!" We looked around dumbfounded. I was completely at odds as to where to start my search for my books.

"Ok my first book is for Psychology 101. Where the fuck do I start?" I looked for a person in a uniform shirt to help us. Everyone looked as if they had just gotten out of bed. One girl had on Spongebob slippers.

"Did we miss the pajama jammy jam memo?" Corynne laughed as she waved her hands around.

"Apparently we did! You in your sundress and matching sandals are totally overdressed!" I walked up the steps to the second floor. "Maybe they label stuff alphabetically." Corynne walked off in a failed attempt to help me find my books. She was just looking for more people to laugh at.

I walked the aisles and my fingers grazed the spine of each book I walked past. A feeling of melancholy washed over me. I remember one time Jordan and I were sitting on his block staring up at the moon. He kissed me on my neck and said to me,

"Always shoot for the moon babygirl, ya hear me?"

"I'm good, I got money and as long as I have it you will too. I don't have to aim for anything baby."

"Money don't last always. If you shoot for the moon and you miss, ya gonna land amongst the stars. Well at least that's what my mom says."

"*You were so right Jordan,*" I said to myself shaking off the memory. A book fell from the shelf and startled me. Corynne came rushing over to me with a look of complete disgust on her face.

"We don't fit in here! Can we please ditch this place?"

"Let me grab my books and supplies Corynne, damn."

"Come on Londyn! You're not really going to do this school shit are you? What are you fucking the dean for then?" I grabbed Corynne by the arm and turned her towards me.

"Lower your voice. Just help me find my shit."

"You want my help? Perfect!" Corynne grabbed my Vuitton wallet and peeled off five one hundred dollar bills. She walked down the steps over to a boy who looked like he was the president of the pocket protector club. "You hey you! You're poor right?'

"Excuse me?" Pocket protector boy said confused as hell.

"I mean you like shop at Wal-Mart and you like buy on sale right?"

"Uh not all the time."

"Yea, yea sure you don't. I recognize a welfare recipient when I see one. Any who, I'll give you five hundred dollars to get the books and supplies on this list and deliver them to this address." Corynne lifted a pen from his pocket, snatched his sleeve up and began writing on his arm.

"What are you doing Cory?"

"Shut up Londyn I'm getting us out of this manual labor, we already spent too much time in here."

"Whatever." I said walking towards the door.

"Ok lil Walmart dude look, do you know who she is?" Corynne pointed in my direction.

"No." Pocket protector looked really nervous.

"She's Londyn Taliaferro."

"As In..."

"Yes as in the mafia princess, fuck around if you want to." Corynne blew a kiss at him and walked towards the door.

"Now come on lets go do something useful like get our nails done." She locked her arm with mine and we stepped out into the sunshine.

Chapter 6

Sergio

Darkness loomed in the distance as I charged down the alleyway towards my target. A voice crackled through my Nextel walkie talkie.

"Sergio he's at the end of the alleyway, we're right behind ya."

"Alright I got his ass," I said as the street lights flickered on and off over head.

The putrid smell of rotting garbage and hot piss made my eyes water. I stood over my mark. He slept soundly encased in layers of tattered clothing, hugging a U-Haul box like it was his long lost lover.

"Ay, Sergio what we's gonna do to this homeless fuck," said Ivan as he kicked the vagrant.

"We's gonna give him the treatment."

"Boss wants the information that bad," the other enforcer, Mike said as we grabbed the homeless man and brought him to his feet.

"Yea apparently he gave a fuck about Londyn's moulie boyfriend."

"Go figure!" Ivan said smacking the transient in the face.

"WAKE UP!" I swung with all my might and socked him in his stomach. His eyes shot open and a gasp of foul air escaped from between his lips.

"Did you see who killed the black boy in the alley awhile back?" I snatched his hats off and jerked his head backwards. I removed my revolver from my waist and rubbed it across his lips. His eyes pleaded with me as if I was God and this was his judgment day.

"Sir I know nothing, I know nothing. Please sir." His eyes were as green as freshly printed money.

"Shut the fuck up! You saw something, what the fuck was it?" I traced the outline of his upper body with the gun. Although he could not feel the coldness of the steel through all the layers of clothing his body still stiffened. "Open your mouth."

Ivan came behind him and tried to pry his mouth open but he clenched his jaws tighter as Ivan dug into the sides of his face.

"You will tell us who shot that boy in the back of his head."

"Sergio I thought he was shot from the front."

"Front, back, side who gives a fuck?"

I pinched the homeless man's nose so that he would have to open his mouth to take a breath. The moment he did I slid my gun between his lips.

"Suck on it." Tears streamed from his eyes and down his face.

"You're crying? You little fucking cock sucker! Just tell me what I need to know!"

"Yea you don't want our boss to come down here!" Ivan pinned his arms behind him. I leaned into him, removed the gun from his mouth and used it to wipe the tears from his face. I looked down at the concrete beneath the homeless man's legs, where a puddle was forming.

"You pissed, you fucking bastard!" I smacked him with butt of the gun. A gash instantly formed.

"Ya scared fella," Ivan said looking down and stepping to the side so the piss wouldn't touch his shoes. I placed the gun at the base of his chin and pulled the trigger. The click of an empty chamber echoed the alley. The homeless man fell to his knees and balled up into the fetal position. We kicked and beat him mercilessly. I tried my hardest to beat through his body with every single blow. I was just about to start pistol whipping the now bloody pulp that lay before me, when I was startled by the ringing of my phone.

"Yea boss we're here."I stepped away from the homeless man. "He doesn't know shit. We tried everything."

Londyn

After hours the registration hall appeared ghostly, lit only by security lamps and track lighting. Donald called me to his office. The little secretary lady was already gone for the evening when I walked past her desk to his office door. *"I wonder why he's still at work at 10:30, don't the offices close at 3?"*

"Hey baby," I walked over to Donald who was seated behind his desk studying a mound of paperwork. I took a seat in front of his desk and crossed my legs.

"Hello beautiful, hows my little pussy cat?" He growled and licked his tongue out at me. It turned my stomach. *"He's so corny,"* I thought.

"Well, I went to get my books earlier today. My classes start next week. I don't have to go right?"

"Of course you have to go."

"What do you mean, baby? I thought we had an arrangement. I've enrolled but I don't have to do anything. It was just so my father would get off my back."

"Babydoll, I can't pad your entire college career. I'm going to need you to do some work."

"Well, I'm not cut out for school work."

"There are student workshops and labs to assist you if you are having trouble, there are also tutors on campus." I stood up, and in a flash I was beside Donald at his desk. I spun him around so he was facing me.

"Do you know who I am and what I do? You must have forgotten. Let me give you a refresher." I fingered his belt, undid the snap on his pants and freed my willing participant from its cotton imprisonment. "Let me taste it baby." Donald groaned as I took him into my mouth.

"You're a God damn pro, baby doll." He muttered as I pressed my lips to the base of his dick, sucked back and swallowed hard. The tension in his thighs began to build as he grew closer and closer to climax with each stroke and flick of my tongue. I held the tip of his dick in my mouth and squeezed tightly. It drove him wild. He was about to scream out when we were both startled by a noise in the hallway.

"Shit, get under the desk!" He said to me as I slid under his desk with his dick still between my lips. I could hear the door turning and someone walking into the office.

"Hello dear, what are you doing out so late?"

"Donald it's Friday, you know I go for martinis with Anastasia and the other country club wives."
Fuck! It's his wife, isn't this a bitch! I hope the bitch doesn't see my purse in the chair. FUCK FUCK FUCK!!" I held onto his dick in my mouth and tried to remain as quiet as possible. I am so not up for getting into any bullshit this evening.

"Oh Paulette I completely forgot about that! Did you enjoy yourself?" The sheer nervousness in his voice pissed me off. *"He's gonna get us caught up!"*

Paulette must have turned her back or she was looking around. He took the opportunity to zip up his pants.

"It's fine honey you've been forgetting about a lot lately. So I was riding by and saw your car, why are you at the office so late?"

"As you can see I have a mountain of work here to tackle and I was trying to get this all done so I didn't have to bring it home."

"Ok well, I'll see you at home, honey. I was just worried. Don't be much longer."

"I won't dear. I promise." I could hear his wife, Paulette walking out of the office. Donald made sure she was a safe distance away before allowing me to come out from underneath the desk.

"Ok like I never want to go through that again," I said taking a deep breath.

"Baby doll, I'm so sorry. She doesn't normally pop up."

"Well she did today, I need to go get a drink, this was a bit much! Call me tomorrow." I grabbed my purse and took the stairs to my car. I was going straight to Fiso's to down a Sex on a Pool Table, and lose myself in the music.

Paulette

"That little bitch was in my husband's office!" I screamed and banged my hands on the steering wheel of my pearl white Audi A6. When I crossed the room to his desk I could smell that same perfume I smelled on him the other night. Then her purse was right on the chair! I drove home in a daze. I stopped to get ice cream. *"This will make me feel a little better."* I sat in the driveway of our home shoveling Moosetracks and pralines into my mouth.

"The nerve of that fucking bastard. We have a life. We have built this together, but fine if he wants to play the game that way, we can. When it's all said and done, it will be my check and check mate."

***

Sunday evening found me stirring up a pot of seafood jambalaya and sipping Chianti from our private reserve. Donald loves my jambalaya, there has never been a time he hasn't demolished every plate I set before him. He'd been gone all day golfing and I wanted to try to have a nice, romantic dinner. *"Maybe I just need to pay him some more attention,"* I thought to myself as I tossed freshly ground cumin into my pot of bubbly goodness. I turned the fire on low and went to shower.

I closed my eyes and imagined Donald's hands caressing me. His touch is so soft. I use to cry when he made love to me. He would look at me as if I was the only woman in the world. I suddenly felt inadequate.

"Why are you doing this to us Donald? Don't you know I love you?" I shouted over the roar of the shower. I finished up in the shower and put on the sexiest nightie I could find in my size. I had gone to

Nine West and purchased the sluttiest looking pair of heels I could find. "If it's a slut he wants, then a slut he will get," I said to myself as I strapped my shoes on. I steadied myself; I haven't been in four inch heels in 15 years! I bought Versace Blonde perfume because the girl at the counter said it was what she wore and she looked like a slut too. So I figured it would do the job. I even went and got a tan. I looked so much better and I felt so good. I hoped he would approve. I pinned my hair up and did my make-up. I returned downstairs to finish preparing my meal when I heard Donald come in.

"Hello honey! I have your favorite on the stove. It's almost ready. I'm sure you're hungry, being out in the sun all day golfing. Come have a seat." I held the seat out for him at the head of the dining room table. He approached me with a puzzled look on his face.

"I'm not hungry dear. What do you have on?"

"Oh this? It's nothing really I just thought you may like if I sex it up a trifle for you."

"Sex it up? What gave you the impression I wanted you to do that?"

"I'm just trying to keep you interested Donald. You don't sleep with me so I'm trying to be innovative. THAT'S ALL!" I walked into the kitchen to turn off the food. I felt tears welling up in my eyes but I fought them back hard.

"Paulette, having sex with you became a chore a long time ago. You took all the fun out of it with all the fertility and invitro nonsense."

"Nonsense Donald? Nonsense? Trying to create a family is nonsense to you? I am so sorry I wanted to have your baby like normal wives want to do for their husbands." I began to wash the dishes feverishly. Cleaning distracts me.

"We are far from normal Paulette. You're barren and I'm shooting almost blank rounds. We are not normal. We weren't meant to be parents." The words from his mouth stung like snake venom. He'd never said those words to me in such a hurtful manner.

"I'm sorry Donald! I'm sorry I'm trying to be romantic, I'm sorry I can't have your baby, or be a good wife! What more do you want from me? You can't get blood from a stone!" My tears begged to be released with each word I spoke. I turned around to look my husband in the face and he was on his way back out the door.

"I'm going back out. I don't have to deal with this." The sound of our front door slamming shook me to my core.

"Fine." I sunk onto the floor in the kitchen and broke down. Tears fell from my eyes and I did nothing to stop them. I was losing my husband and while I had no confirmation he was cheating on me, I could feel his soul taking back the part of his heart he had given me when we took our marriage vows.

***

Chapter 7

Londyn

Scores of people crowded in front of Ms. Latrice's tiny house on Newkirk Street. The sun beat down on the pavement as I made my way through the door. The bidding had begun for valuable items within the walls of the only home Jordan had ever known. I walked in unnoticed by his mother who was on her way out the back door. I quickly made my way to the front of the living room where the auctioneer was making his arrangements with various potential customers.

"Excuse me sir. What's the cost of the back taxes?"

"Im sorry ma'am?"

"Ok maybe it's a little early, but I need to know how much to pay off the entire debt on this property."

"Well the total debt owed we are attempting to accumulate is $37,327.00."

"I'd like to pay that off. I'd also like you to give a refund to whoever has already purchased items. I'll be buying those as well."

"Yes ma'am!"

I cut the check for the required amount and made my way out back. Jordan's mother was staring off into the distance. Her cigarette was trembling on the edge of her lip. Tears rolled down her face as I put my hand on her shoulder.

"Lord what am I going to do? My husband bought me this house. It's all I have. James is gone, Jordan's gone. I spent all my money burying them both. What am I going to do?" Her voice quivered with each word she spoke.

"Ms. Latrice, your house is fine. I love you and I love Jordan. I would never see you put out of your home. I paid what was owed to the city. They won't bother you anymore."

Ms.Latrice turned around and wrapped her arms around my neck hugging me tightly as if she had just won the lottery. She stepped back and took a good look at me. I adjusted my mini skirt in an attempt to look a little more presentable. She frowned.

"Londyn what is going on with you? You don't seem like the same child who came around her every day with my son. You've changed. What's wrong?"

"Nothing is wrong- I just don't care anymore, love left me. So what do I have?" Ms. Latrice grabbed me by the chin, and looked me square in the eye.

"What do you have? What do you have? My God little girl you have breath, life, legs to walk, eyes to see, and hands to feel your way around! Don't you dare say what do you have!"

"But Ms.Latrice I'm so..." She cut me off before I could finish my sentence.

"Enough with the pity parties and woe is me days. Jordan wouldn't want you to be so depressed about his passing. Just look at you. You giving the best lil' hoes on the strip a run for they money."

"I know. I know."

"Well do something about it. Crazy as my son was he would come out his grave and kick your behind for what you wearing right now. Get it together, before you end up on the news as well." She kissed me on my cheek. The love in her eyes was unmistakable. I started to ask her what else she needed for the house, but I turned my head and saw Honor coming through the kitchen.

"Ms. Trice, I'm not trying to go through drama with Honor today, I'm leaving." I kissed her on her forehead. "Call me if you need anything please."

"I will daughter, I will." I ran down the steps of the back porch, through the back yard and out of the gate. I rounded the corner out of the alley way behind her house.

"What the fuck am I doing," I thought as I pulled off of Jordan's block. *"This whore shit is for the birds."*

Giuseppe

"Mr. Taliaferro, good morning. Mr. Dockens and the members of the board would like to meet with you in the board room sir," Alyssa, my receptionist, said to me as I walked past her desk into my office.

"I already know what that's about Ms. Davis. Thank you very much." I dropped my briefcase in my office and proceeded down the hall to my boardroom. *"More propaganda and bullshit, I swear if I didn't have to have a board to maintain this business I'd fire all these fucks."*

Staunch and stoic was the mood when I entered my boardroom. All the board members looked about 80 years old- all white and all avoided trouble whenever possible.

"Ah Giuseppe, so good to see you again." Stanley Frapp shook my hand as I took my seat.

"Always my pleasure Stanley. How was Aruba? I trust you found my bungalow to your liking?"

"Beautiful as always."

"Good I'm pleased then. Now what is this impromptu meeting about gentleman?"

"Well Mr.Taliaferro, in light of recent court room events we as your board of trustees had to convene to see if it was in the best interest of the company to allow you to stay at it's helm." Patrick Oswald looked like he was pleased with himself. My blood began to boil. I built my company from the ground up. I did everything the right way- not one dirty cent was ever invested into Taliaferro and Associates. I made sure of that. My law practice is business, and my mafia business is personal. Never the twain shall meet.

"Enlighten me Patrick. What courtroom events are you speaking of?"

"Let's not be coy Giuseppe. An elderly woman shoots the star witness and herself in one of your mob buddies' cases." Patrick looked as if steam was rising from his collar.

"I'm sorry I don't know anyone in the mob personally. I've represented several members of different crime organizations; however that is what I do. Are you accusing me of something?"

"We know you orchestrated the events in the courtroom last week." Augustus Olivero stood and stared me down as if to try to shake me at my core. I rose to my feet and walked slowly to the head of my conference table.

"Let me make something very clear for all of you. I am a lawyer. I am the best damn criminal attorney this side of the Atlantic. I do not, nor have I ever had any criminal ties. Who I represent is business. Don't make assumptions based on the media frenzy that was created." I walked to the boardroom door and swung it open holding it steady with my left hand. "Please understand this is my company at the end of the day. I handpicked each of you for my board for specific reasons. I will replace those who I don't see having the best interest of me and my company at heart. I am the CEO, COO, CFO and all other titles in between. Don't get on my bad side gentlemen, good day." I motioned for the board members to exit with my right hand. Each left in silence. I instantly felt the tension growing at the base of my neck. I grabbed my briefcase and headed back out of the office.

"Ms. Davis, I'll be at the cigar lounge if you need me. Send me a message on my blackberry if it is of great importance."

"Yes sir, Mr. Taliaferro sir."

I stepped into the elevator, loosened up the French knot in my tie. *"First Londyn, now this trustee shit. What's next?"*

Paulette

"Donald will you please grab my 9 iron from the trunk. It must have fallen out." Today is our monthly couples golf game. The Bennetts, the Torans, and ourselves play 18 holes of golf. It's normally great fun, but I'm still reeling from my unsuccessful attempt at a romantic dinner.

"Yes dear I'll get it." Donald looked less than pleased that he had to spend time with me today. "I hope this doesn't take all day, I have paperwork to attend to."

"I'm sure you have things to attend to, but I'm quite certain it isn't paperwork."

"Excuse me? What did you say?"

"Nothing Donald let's just try to get through the afternoon in peace." The Bennets were single handedly the two happiest black people I've ever met in my life. Eboni and Tony seemed to live the perfect life. He is a war veteran and high ranking officer in the army. She's a marine biologist. Along with their two children they look like the poster family for suburban America; except for the fact they both have extreme drinking habits. The Torans are at bit more dysfunctional. Adele is a pill popping CPA and Craig is a doctor who screws his maid on the regular. *"No wonder my marriage is falling apart. Look at the company we keep!"* I took my seat in the golf cart beside the only man I've ever loved. He looked at me in disgust. I rolled my eyes and sighed loudly. "What else is new?"

"What are you talking about Paulette?" Donald snapped his head around. It seemed like every word I spoke irritated him to no end.

"Ah Paulette, Donald! We weren't sure you were going to make it. How goes things?" Craig extended his hand to Donald and firmly shook it.

"We're good Craig, how's the practice?"

"It's coming along nicely now. How are things in academia?"

"Slow and steady as she goes. Shall we golf?" The summer breeze blew my red curls two and fro as we approached the 8th hole. As Donald approached the green I quickly ran up behind him and gave him a hug.

"I love you. I want to make us work, let's go to counseling darling." His back became rigid as he readied himself to swing his club. "Counseling will not save what is left of this situation. There is no us." Donald's ball landed just short of the 8th hole. He picked up his golf bag and walked off the course.

"Donald! Donald come back here!" I tried to run to catch up with him as fast as my tubby little legs would carry me. I gave up. What's the use?

"To hell with this game today! Anyone up for a glass of wine?" I could hear Tony say faintly as I continued to walk off the course. *"I tried, Donald I really have tried. All is fair in love and war."*

***

After a long and trying day on the golf course I tried to shower the afternoon's embarrassment off of me. I had driven us to the golf course and when I left I could have cared less how Donald was going to get back home. He was both inconsiderate and inept. The nerve of him. At least if he were going to carry on an affair he should do it with discretion as most men do. I heard the muffled purring of a midlife crisis pull into the drive way. It was only 8pm, Donald was home earlier then he had been most nights. He bounded up the steps smiling from ear to ear with a bundle of lilies in his hand. I was seated on the edge of our bed slathering lotion on my hog sized thighs. He laid the flowers down beside me and was humming some unrecognizable tune.

"I'm sorry about earlier dear. Let me make it up to you. Donald took a few squirts of the creamy aromatic goodness and warmed it in his hands. The feeling I got as he rubbed his hands across my back was one of pure bliss. His slow deliberate kisses as the nape of my neck excited me. I shifted my heaviness back and forth as he ran his still lotioned hands up and down my body. My inner thighs pulsated with anticipation. Donald's legs nearly burst at the hips straddling me. I lay back prepping myself to receive what I had been waiting for what seemed like eons. He pulled down the strap of my nightie and cupped my breast in his mouth. The sleeve of his golf shirt brushed past my nose as he ran his fingers through my hair. I caught a whiff of the same perfume I had smelled on him before.

"Donald..." I managed to moan to between passionate stomach turning kisses.

"Yes, love?" Donald tore his shirt off and the bareness of his chest turned me on even more.

"My love, I hate to ask you again, but who wears that perfume? I keep smelling it on you." Donald jumped up taken aback that I even asked him a question like that. He grabbed my legs and pulled me to him.

"I just want to make love Paulie, no questions, just us." He kissed me deeply, and I let all my questions fall by the way side. He is my husband after all. Donald entered me and I immediately felt the curve in his shaft on my g-spot. He stroked in and out, which drove me wild! Once I was nearly at my climax he began to rub his thumb on my clitoris. I felt my rolls

51

begin to vibrate and I knew I was surely about to orgasm. Donald could feel it as well, he slowed his stroke and removed himself from me, immediately inserting his two fingers.

"Donald what are you doing?" My breath became labored as I'm sure something was about to happen to me that had never happened before.

Donald kept his fingers inside me and began to suck on my breast, he quietly whispered to me "It's ok Paulie, just let it happen." What happened next was of epic proportions. Donald rubbed my g-spot until I thought I was going to burst, and then quickly removed his fingers causing me to orgasm more than I ever have! All over the bed and smack in the middle of Donald's chest like it was a bull's-eye. I was spent, the room was spinning and I was at its axis. Donald in all of our years of marriage had never fucked me with such voracity and fervor. I was convinced now more than ever that he was sleeping with someone else. I was determined to figure this out. There is no amount of mind blowing sex that will deter me from my quest. He was surely fucking some slut. He didn't learn those tricks on Pornstar.com.

Chapter 9

Londyn

The sound of the alarm clock crept into my dream. I dreamt Jordan and I were running a race against each other. The alarm buzzer was our signal to go. Racing over time and through space to get to each other. "I'M COMING JORDAN I WON'T LEAVE YOU BEHIND!" I screamed out waking myself up from the dream. I turned to look at the clock. "7:30, fuck it's too early for this shit. How am I supposed to function, let alone learn at this time of morning?"

I quickly showered and dressed. My first day as a college student started at 8:30, it was going to take me at least a half an hour to get into the city to the campus. Throwing my netbook into my hobo bag I grabbed the book I needed for my morning class and ran across the courtyard to grab a bagel before heading out of the door.

***

Butterflies danced in my stomach as I pulled into the student assigned parking lot. "8:16 cool... I guess I can wander around and figure out where the hell I'm going!'

As I walked up the steps to Caulder, the building that housed my first class, I tripped and my book fell out in front of me on the steps. "Fuck!" I screamed.

"Here let me get that for you."

"Oh, well thank you. My name is Londyn."

"I know who you are. My name is Allen." Allen bent over to grab my book and help me up quickly. Tall and lanky he looked like the poster child for the gothic movement. Much browner than myself, he had really long dreads twisted neatly to his scalp and cropped into some knot in the back of his head.

Hazel brown eyes peered back at me from behind 80's style eye glasses. Not at all my type but something was completely intriguing about him.

"Sometimes I forget my face is always in the damn paper." I said as I sized him up. Do you know where Mr. Harris's class is?"

"Sure I'll walk you there. No big deal." As we walked up the steps and through the doors Allen touched the door knob four or five times before holding it open for me. "Don't mind me, I have OCD. "

"Eww, what is that?"

"It's a disorder. I don't want to talk about it." He looked up and down and from right to left so often I thought his head was going to spin.

"Ok whatever, look thanks for picking my stuff up. I guess I'll see you around." I raced up the remaining steps and left Allen at the bottom of the step. *"Ok he was weird as hell, cute but super creepy."*

***

Everyone looked so much smarter than me when I entered into the class and took my seat near the back. *"I hope I don't fall asleep."*

"Good morning ladies and gentlemen. I am Mr. Harris and today is the beginning of the change in perception of how you see everything from this point on." I was completely enthralled. As he pointed at charts and graphs and we turned page after page in our book I couldn't believe he was holding my attention! The class ended and I took a look at my watch 10:00 am... it didn't even seem like I had been sitting still for an hour and a half. As I gathered my things and exited the class room I felt my phone buzzing on my hip. It was Javier, the cardiac surgeon calling for his weekly date with me.

"Hola, mi amor, I can't wait to see you today."

"Hey Javier what's up? I just got out of class, where are you?"

"I'm over on Cobbs Creek Parkway headed to the countryside. Where are you? Want me to pick you up?"

"No that wouldn't be a good idea, daddy saw your Aston Martin drop me off the other week and he was livid. He's so overprotective. Meet me at the Hilton on 11th and Arch. I learned some new yoga moves I want to show you."

"I can't wait mi amor." Javier whispered into the phone in his sexiest, non-sexy voice.

"Yea, I'm so sure." I slid my thumb across my iPhone to release the call. "Fuck I'm not going all the way home, I'll grab some Le pearla panties from Saks on City line."

Javier Castillo was a closet freak. I could only imagine what his wife would do if she knew all of the things he was into. He liked me to take my panties and put them in his mouth, or there are days he liked to try them on, wanting me to treat him like the woman. I gotta admit, initially putting a strap on and penetrating his ass took a lot out of me. But now? I'm a pro! After grabbing the panties and a pair of heels, I threw them on with my trench coat I keep in my trunk and sped off to the Hilton downtown. Coming down Broad Street I noticed there was a black car that had been following me since the school. *My daddy thinks he's so slick. He can follow me all he wants to, I don't care.*

I looked up again and the black car was gone. I parked and made my way into the hotel. Javier was excitedly waiting in the lobby for me.

"Are you ready for me papi?" I said kissing him and leading him towards the elevators.

"I've been waiting mi amor. I am so ready..."

***

After I gave Javier what he needed I was feeling a little guilty.

"Since when did I get a conscience?"

As I was leaving the hotel I stopped at the liquor store in the lobby and grabbed a bottle of Captain Morgan's. Tossing it into my Balenciaga tote I hopped onto the expressway and headed towards Woodlawn Cemetery to visit the only man I know, aside from my father, who has ever had some sort of love for me. Rain started to fall, lightly kissing my skin as I walked over to Jordan's grave. The Captain Morgan's was calling my name. I turned the bottle to my lips praying the rain and alcohol could wash away my sins.

"Jordan why did you have to leave? Why aren't you here?" The silence was so loud I screamed louder.

"WHY AREN'T YOU HERE JORDAN? WHY DID YOU LEAVE ME? I THOUGHT YOU LOVED ME, LOVED US! I WISH I COULD DIE AND BE WITH YOU. IT'S SO HARD WITHOUT YOU HERE..." I took my heels off and sat cross legged in front of his tombstone. I stared at the words in front of me until my vision blurred.

Jordan Tariq Walters

December 20, 1989 – April 28, 2011

Loved by many, but loved by God more.

I wept openly for the first time really since Jordan passed. My sobs echoed through the cemetery filled with those who couldn't hear my cries.

"I'm so lost without you baby. So lost." No response, not even a whisper. "Baby, daddy put me in college. He said I needed to make something of myself. It wasn't bad. I was surprised I didn't fall asleep. I'm trying to do good baby, really I am. I helped mommy keep the house, they were going to take it from her." I stood up and walked to the foot of Jordan's grave. The willow tree next to it bowed to me as I surveyed the cemetery.

"I don't want to be here anymore Jordan. I can't take it. I'm just going to let go Jordan. I can't take it anymore. I just want to die."

Chapter 10

Londyn

I laid by the pool, Chloe sunglasses to mask my dismay. Why am I not as carefree and fun loving as I used to be? I need to fuck somebody. It will make me feel better. As if on cue Tre or Trevor, as my father referred to him, walked past me on his way into the house. His sexy little ass was mine for the taking.

"Hey Tre, would you mind rubbing some suntan lotion on my legs for me please?"

"Good afternoon, Ms. Londyn, umm sure why not." His voice was uncertain as if he should even be looking at, let alone touching, his boss's daughter. I pulled the string on my bikini beneath my towel so there was nothing but pussy and opportunity between me and good, old Tre. His hands nervously slid up my right leg and as he neared the cusp of my inner thigh he paused. I grabbed his hand and rubbed it across my hairless pussy. He looked up at me unsure of what was to come. I grabbed him by his hand wrapped my towel around my waist and quickly led him into the pool house. Once inside the door I pushed him down onto the couch and removed my bathing suit top.

"Ms. Londyn I'm not sure we should be doing this, I'm supposed to be at a meeting with your father in 10 minutes."

"Well how fast can you cum?" I snatched his pants down around his ankles and marveled at the erection before me. Tre' had to be at least 10 ½ inches and it was thick! I was going to have fun trying to fit all of his manliness in me! I used his standard accountant CPA school issued tie to bind his hands so he couldn't touch me. This pleasure was going to be all mine. I slid my wetness down onto his massive dick slowly until my tight little round ass was flesh up against his balls. His eyes danced with excitement as I slow rocked my hips. I reached into the space between the couch pillows and retrieved my hot pink bullet, adjusted the setting from 'warm and fuzzy feeling' to 'motor mouth' and placed it on my clit. Doing this sent a rush of excitement through my body. I slammed down hard onto Tre's dick and with his hands tied he could only moan and clench his butt cheeks as he was surely about to climax. My toes curled and I tossed my head back as my pussy orgasmed uncontrollably. With each spasm of my walls Tre's body shook. Feeling refreshed and so much more like myself. I hopped off of his dick much quicker than I had climbed on.

"You can let yourself out Tre, thanks. Don't be late to your meeting!" I rushed upstairs to shower.

"Hey Londyn wait, you're just going to leave me here with a hard dick?"

"Sorry Tre, that sounds like a personal problem."

Giuseppe

"Where in the hell is Trevor? He's normally always always 15 minutes early!" I barked to myself as I paced back and forth across my office floor.

"THOMAS....THOMAS!" I yelled out into the main part of the house from my office.

"Yes Mr. Taliaferro?" Thomas said quietly as he came into the office.

"I need a new Persian. This rug has got some wear on it. I don't like it anymore. "

"Yes sir, Mr. Taliaferro, I will place the order in the morning."

"Thomas, place the order now, I want a new rug as soon as possible."

"Yes Mr. Taliaferro, sir. " Thomas backed quietly out of the door he had entered in. As he crossed the threshold of the office door, back out into the foyer, Trevor nearly bowled him over.

"My apologies Thomas. Do you forgive me?"

"No worries Mr. Grant."

I looked Trevor up and down and could tell he was noticeably frazzled. It was certainly unlike him to be late.

"Is everything ok Trevor? I see that you were nearly late, when you are almost always 15 minutes early."

"Oh yes Mr. Taliaferro, everything is fine sir. I had Chipotle for lunch and that doesn't seem to agree with me."

"See Trevor, that's why you have to stick to what you know. None of this new-fangled shit. Come have a seat." I motioned for him to take the seat in front of my desk. "Stogie?"

"No sir, Mr. Taliaferro. I think I have mentioned before that I don't smoke."

"Your loss! Now what is this you needed to speak with me about?" A billow of smoke rose from the freshly burning cigar, the inhale filled my lungs.

"Well sir, we need to decide what we are going to do about the company stock. Are we going to allow it to be traded on the open market or are we going to keep it private? Something has to be done. We are at a pivotal point in the company's growth and development. I think that, with the right people behind it, this company could grow to Trump-esque proportions." The excitement in Trevor's voice was clear and apparent.

"Trevor look, I know Trump, I've played golf with him sat down at his table and had a meal. I do not bide my time trying to get to where another man is. I built this company on my back, blood, sweat, and tears. "As I was about to get into a more in depth explanation of the foundation of my law firm, the phone rang.

"Excuse me, Trevor, I need to get this....Hello?" It was the Dean at Londyn's school.

"Hey Giuseppe, it's Donald at the school, I just wanted to hold up my end of our arrangement, just wanted to let you know Londyn attended all of her classes today. No absences."

"Donald, I appreciate the phone call. Thank you for holding up your end of the bargain. I'm in a meeting with my financial advisor now; I'll make sure the school gets that check in a few weeks."

"I can't thank you enough, Giuseppe, really."

"Look Donald, you make sure my daughter passes, does her work and adheres to your policies, I'm not sending her there to skate through. "

"You got it!" I placed the phone back in its cradle and I shifted my attention back to Trevor. "You know what Trevor I have something else to attend to, can you cut a check for 25k to Londyn's school, and make sure you have it written off as a charitable donation. This meeting is over." I pushed back from my desk, extinguished my stogie and walked out of the office leaving Trevor just as flustered and confused as he was when he entered.

Londyn

Sometimes when I'm sitting in my vanity mirror I wonder what it would have been like to grow up with a mom, and play in her make-up and try on her jewelry.

Ah well fuck it. I finished brushing my freshly washed hair and tied it back into a bun. I threw my robe on because I could hear my father's footsteps on my steps.

"Bella... where are you," my father shouted from the steps.

"In here dad." I started applying lotion to my face and arms when he walked in.

"It's really nice in here Bella. I don't come in here too often. Maybe I should stay in here and you can stay in the big house, this is cozy."

"Umm, no daddy I like my little place just fine. What's up, what brings you to my tiny palace?" He came and stood behind me and rested his hands on my shoulders."Bella, I am so proud of you. Actually going to class and doing what is required of you. I just want you to have a little token of my appreciation."

"A new Range Rover?" I said excitedly. I really wanted one too, after all, my car is 18 months old, he doesn't expect me to drive that for much longer does he? *'I'd look sexy in a new truck.'*

"Let's see your grades first before we talk 100k vehicles."

He handed me a purple velvet box. It instantly triggered a memory for me. I knew what was inside of this box. Since I was a little girl my Nonna, my grandmother, kept her blue diamond heart shaped necklace in the box I was holding in my hands. The hinges on the ancient box creaked and groaned as I opened it. It had been 10 years since Nonna passed. I doubt my father opened it since then. I gasped and my eyes welled up with tears as he lifted the necklace from its old home and unfastened the clasp to place it on my neck.

"Now you will have a little piece of Nonna wherever you go." He kissed my forehead and walked out. I held the necklace gently in my hands as the chain became accustomed to its new owner. Tears were still falling uncontrollably from my eyes. Even though my father had given me my grandmother's most prized possession, I was still empty on the inside. Diamonds will never replace Jordan.

Chapter 11

Paulette

As I pursed my lips and sipped my mai tai, my mind was racing. No little umbrella straw in my drink would liven up my day. Donald and I were barely speaking. After that mind blowing sex session I wouldn't let him touch me. So he had taken to sleeping in the guest bed and I couldn't blame him. After all, I am sobbingly fat and disgusting. Sweat poured from beneath the brim of my tiny polka dotted hat as I awaited the arrival of the detective. Though it was September on the east coast it was unseasonably warm. My protruding belly begged to be freed from the cotton confines of my snugly fit sundress. The resounding start and stop of an old model car diverted my attention. An old Chevy pick-up bucked to a stop in front of the Belrose restaurant. I chose the bistro café in King of Prussia because I'd be damned if anyone would interrupt my meeting. I knew too many people in the city and I didn't need those cackling crows in my business. Ted was not your stereotypical detective; he put you to mind of an Italian plumber or meat market owner. His pot belly gave mine a run for its money; his hair clinging to its last hopes of youthfulness was combed over his forehead in a failed attempt to look young. *"Must be a mid-life crisis,"* I thought to myself as I watched him fidget in his pocket attempting to find a quarter or two to feed the money hungry meter. I waddled to the entrance of the restaurant to greet him.

We shook hands and his sweaty palms made me cringe. He wiped his hands on the front of his poorly buttoned shirt and we walked back to the table.

"So nice to finally put a face with a name, Mrs. Jones. I wish I was seeing your very lovely face under a different set of circumstances. However we both know why we are here."

"Yes it is unfortunate that we have to meet like this Mr. Darowich. Were you able to find out anything?
"

"I'm not sure how to say this."

"Just say it, I'm sure I already know." I began to wring my hands in anticipation. '*All these years of marriage for what? For it to end like this? Was this his first affair? Or the first time he got sloppy.*' My mind raced and the air around me became sparse. My eyes darted back and forth. *"God Dammit not an anxiety attack. Not right now, Mary, Mother of God. What the hell!"*

"Mrs. Jones, are you ok? " Ted looked concerned as he pulled out the manila envelope. The red ribbon that bound the material was all that was left holding together the fragile pieces of my now shattered marriage.

"I'm fine, Ted please show me the documents."

"Well as you can see here from his EZ Pass records he's made quite a few trips over the same bridge in New Jersey at 2 and 3 in the morning. With the access you gave me I downloaded his points of origin from his GPS. Four times he has been to the same Plainfield, New Jersey hotel. I'm sure he's not in the dog house that bad that he has to go to Jersey ta find a decent place to lay his head ya know?"

"Please continue." A sob welled in my throat and I fought back with all the power I had in my tiny chubby body.

"I have pictures would you like to see them? They are a bit graphic."

"Yes please." And just that fast, there it was in front of me like black and white splattered all over a newspaper. There was the red all over, Donald and his slut fucking on the balcony of some hotel in New Jersey. The look on her face was one of pure enjoyment and ecstasy. I tried to stand up to walk away from the table, away from the harsh reality that had just been handed to me in my lap. As I pushed away from the table, I felt my lower extremities give up, the same way Donald gave up on our marriage.

"Someone call an ambulance! This lady has passed out!" I could faintly hear Ted screaming at the wait staff.

Londyn

In the passing weeks meeting Allen had become more frequent. I was learning to tolerate his super weirdness. He called it OCD, I just called it fucking retarded. He always spoke in circles and riddles and puzzles. Which at times got on my nerves but it was teaching me some words I didn't know.

"Allen, I'm not too sure about school. I mean I like it and all but what the hell. All this work!"

"Now, Miss Londyn, you have to realize the enormity of the ramifications if you should choose to discontinue your matriculation."

"HUNH?" I blankly stared at Allen awaiting his translation.

"Plainly put my striking muse, you should stay in school."

"Ok then Allen why don't you just say that. You don't have to use super big words all the time, damn."

"My apologies if my poeticness offends you Miss Londyn."

"Whatever Allen." I loosely thumbed the pages of my text book. My phone began ringing *"5/12 in boys ass is off the hook, Cinderella bout to lose the glass off her foot."* "That's Cory, give me a minute Allen let me see what she wants." I slid my thumb across my touch screen to answer the phone. Allen busied himself in some metaphysics book, tracing the outlines of the words as he read. *"So cute and weird,"* I thought to myself. I excused myself from our table and ran out of the front door of the library to see what Cory was up to.

"What's up hooker."

"Bitch, oh em gee, guess what! Where are you at?"

"Girl what? I'm studying with Allen at the library." I could see a few guys out of the corner of my eye; eyeing my ass as I stood in front of the library pivoting from one foot to the other. *"I need a tan,"* I thought while Corynne was running her mouth.

"Juan got me tickets for us to go see Young Money in concert tonight!" Corynne's excitement jumped through the phone.

"I don't know if I can do tonight. I'm supposed to see D (my code name for the dean) tonight. And Allen and I are studying."

"Bitch I know you didn't tell me you are passing up a chance to see Young Money in concert to roll around with some old dick and a retard? Get the fuck out of here! I'm pulling up right now you're going to have to tell me this shit to my face."

Londyn looked up and Corynne's peanut butter brown Lexus sc 450 zoomed around the bend into the parking lot.

Corynne's Coachella shirt dress hugged her in all the right places and her hair flowed in the breeze.

"Now, what you say bitch?" Corynne flipped her sunglasses onto the top of her head and flung her Marc Jacobs hobo back onto her shoulder.

"Girl just come in here and sit with me for a minute then we can go get something to eat."

"Don't try to bribe me with food. Hurry up you know we have to go find something to wear!"

Back at the table Allen was still busy looking over text books and his oversized earphones played some heavy bass beat. He bobbed his head inside the little world where he was king as Corynne and I came back to the table. I startled Allen when I tapped him to introduce him to Corynne. His hands flew up in complete fear and defense. Corynne burst into a fit of giggles.

"I'm sorry if I scared you Allen. I just wanted you to meet my friend Corynne."

Allen stood up and held out a chair for Corynne. "It is my most humble pleasure to make your acquaintance Miss Corynne." Allen held his hand out for Corynne to shake it but she just looked at him with disgust and sat down.

"Seriously Londyn, how much more time do we have to waste here with the rain man? He's giving me hives." Corynne cringed as Allen reached to offer her a spring water from his back pack. "No thanks buddy. I ONLY DRINK IMPORTED WATER. I DON'T WANT YOUR WELFARE WATER. THANKS ANYWAY."

"Cory, seriously? He was just being nice." I looked at her like she was crazy. I get that Allen isn't on our level. But he is the nicest person I met at school so far.

"Well being nice has never gotten me anywhere." Corynne scoffed.

"Miss Corynne I regret that the libations I have offered you are not suitable enough for a woman of your caliber. Perhaps I can go and purchase you some that would be to your liking?" Allen hung his head and is eyes darted back and forth as he waited in anticipation for Corynne's response.

"Whatever the fuck that means. Look Londyn are you coming with or what? You can waste your day with this weirdo if you want to. But I have things to do to get ready for the concert. You know this school shit is only to get your dad off your back, so really, stop tripping. When you come to your senses, I'll be at the car." Corynne pushed her chair back and stomped off to her car like a wife who had made a final demand of her husband.

"Allen I am so sorry for her behavior! I will call you later ok?"

"I shall bid you adieu until I see your sweet, lovely face again."

"BYE!" I huffed, and gathered my books quickly. I rushed out to Corynne's car. What was I supposed to do? She was my BFF after all.

Donald

I was perusing the web for places to take my little darling on vacation when Marjorie; my secretary rang my phone.

"Sir, I don't want to alarm you but you wife has been rushed to the hospital."

"Oh my, the hospital for what?"

"If I knew that I'd be a mind reader. I am just relaying the message sir. Not that you're really all that worried about your wife anyway."

"Excuse me. She's my wife, I love her."

"Oh I thought you had traded her in for a new younger more I-talian model."

"You need to mind your business Majorie." I slammed the phone down and grabbed my briefcase.

"I can text my sweetie and tell her tonight is a no go. I have to make sure Paulette is ok first."

As I dashed through the city in my car my mind was wrought with fear. *"Had I done something to make Paulette sick? Was my affair causing her undue stress? Did she know about the affair and do something to harm herself?"* When my car came to a blaring halt in front of the emergency room door at Ben Franklin Hospital I rushed into the waiting room and up to the receptionists desk.

"My wife was brought in, Paulette Jones. Please can you tell me if she's ok."

"Sir she's in room 7. You may go in."

To me it took forever to get to room 7 in the back of the emergency room. I don't know if my feet just wouldn't carry me or if it was the fact that I was terrified to see what could have possibly happened to her. I took the seat beside her bed and grabbed her hand. Still fast asleep from the sedative she stirred a bit when I kissed her hand.

"Paulie, I know I haven't been to you who I needed to be. I just need you to be ok."

I stayed there with her. I needed her to be ok. Just because I am often short and distant with her, doesn't mean that I don't love her. *"I need to do a better job of taking care of home."*

I must have dozed off because the sun was setting as Paulette came to.

"Oh Donald. How long have I been out dear?" She reached to see what was tethering her to the bed as she reached out to try and hug me.

"Just rest darling. I'm glad you are ok."

"I don't know what happened. I was at lunch and the next thing I knew I was here."

"The doctors are running tests now. I've called your mother and I will keep them posted. Just relax."

"Thank you for coming."

"I don't know what I would have done if something happened to you. I know I have been an ass lately, and you have been a pill. However that doesn't change the fact that I would never want anything bad to happen to you." The truth in my words weighed heavy on me and sunk to the pit of my stomach like a faulty buoy.

Chapter 12

Londyn

Sometimes I fear sleep, so I stay up and party all night because then when I finally do fall asleep, I may not remember. Night after night I had the same dream. I would fight my sleep only to awaken drenched in sweat and realizing that there is nothing I can do to change what happened.

The gutteral wailings of a soul tied from mother to son, broken by a life cut down too short could be heard from the entryway of the church. Her pain echoed to the rafters as she made her way with the rest of her family behind her to lay to rest her son, her baby son, her child who doctors said wasn't going to make it while she was delivering him. Her knees buckled and her eldest son and her brother had to hold her up. If she could have switched places surely she would have placed herself inside the mahogany casket instead of a child, her child, who had so much to live for. No resolution, no motive, only pain. The hood of the casket swayed back and forth as Honor and his other cousins filed in one by one. As the casket adornment was removed and they prepared the casket to close, Ms. Latrice stood up, threw her hands to the high heavens, and passed out.

The buzzing of my phone woke me up. A tear escaped my eye as I sat up to answer.

"This is me." I muttered still half asleep.

"Bitch it's me, I know you aren't asleep!"

"Corynne, I do have class in the morning."

"Will you come off the school shit, seriously. What the fuck? Anyway, Juan wants you to meet his brother, Mannix. He has a wife or whatever but since when did that ever matter? They want to take us to Barbados on Friday."

"Cory, I can't go. I'm really starting to get over this shit."

"What the fuck Londyn, it's just getting to be fun. But whatever, more dick for me." I hung up.

Maybe she just wasn't getting it. Or maybe school was changing me. I got up to shut my window, the cold breeze blowing through my room made my nipples hard. I reached into my nightstand and grabbed my dildo.

"Mmmm," I caught my breath as I ground my hips down on to my imaginary lover. Its 5 speed random vibe action always caused me to orgasm quicker than I could shove it into my pussy. My body shook as my clit danced up and down in sheer enjoyment of my masturbation. I imagined Jordan's arms wrapped around me. No hands felt as good as his, as strong as his. He fit inside me just right. No man will ever make me feel the way he did.

Giuseppe

The marble floor sounded hollow as I paced back and forth in my bedroom. It was rare that I got a full night's rest. I headed down to the kitchen to make myself a sandwich and gather my thoughts.

"Dammit, I wish I could get you off my mind."

"Mr. Taliaferro are you ok?" Rosie said quietly as she emerged from the laundry room with two baskets of freshly washed sheets.

"Rosie, I'm fine. Did I ever tell you the story of how I met my first love?" I motioned for Rosie to have a seat next to me. "Odd how Londyn's mother and I got together. She was a dancer for the Alvin Ailey dance company and they came to town for a performance. Ma asked me to accompany her for the evening and when I saw her I was fascinated. Her skin was the most beautiful shade of brown I had ever seen. Her legs went on for days. She was graceful, and poised. I had to have her. I had Louis, the family runner at the time, advise her that the son of Abenzio Taliaferro would like to have dinner with her after the show. She obliged. I was only 18 but man I'll tell ya I was head over heels in love with her. Ms. Rebecca Scott. I caught hell from Ma and Pa when I explained to them, after only a week of spending time together, I was hell bent on giving her my grandmother's 15 carat emerald and diamond engagement ring. I was ready to be disowned by my family. When I looked into Rebecca's eyes I only saw her, not black or white."

"It sounds like you really did love her Mr. Taliaferro sir. Might I ask what happened?"

"I think her only flaws were, that one, she loved me and, two, she was born black."

"Que?" Rosie's eye brows furrowed looking for more information from me.

"Ma and Pa were furious. As old school Italians you marry your own kind. No offense to you but Ma always said you don't run around with the help."

"I don't take no offense to that Mr.Taliaferro, Latino's are the same way, we stick together."

"Ok, so you understand where my parents were coming from."

"Si."

"Three months into our relationship I was ordered to break it off with Rebecca. She was in New York finishing up the run of the show and then she had plans to move to Philadelphia and I was going to buy her a studio to teach dance lessons. Before I could call to tell her I couldn't see her any more she called me from a pay phone in 30th Street Station. She had been ejected from the show. She was pregnant."

Rosie got up to pour me a glass of bourbon; I found it oddly comforting to confide in her. I hadn't talked about Rebecca openly in years.

"I quickly went to pick her up, and brought her back here to the estate. With my mother and father both seated in the parlor we told them she was pregnant; that I was the father and we planned on being together. My mother fainted. My father shot a look across the room at me. His eyes were like daggers. He stood up to leave, turned to me, and said, 'Correggi il tuo mess, sbarazzarsi di questa nigger.' Simply put, he told me to get rid of Rebecca and fix my mistake."

I paused not sure if I wanted to continue. Rosie put her hand on my shoulder to assure me I could go on.

"I refused to dispose of Rebecca or our child. I moved out of this house, the only home I'd ever known. Rebecca and I got married. When Londyn was three months old my father was gunned down. I immediately had to assume control of my family, my mother demanded I choose. My family or my 'moulie' as she put it. I wrote Rebecca a check for $100k, kept Londyn and sent her mother away forever. I'll never forgive myself. It keeps me up most nights. I've never loved again."

"Well Mr. Taliaferro, sir, what I can say is that I know you love this woman, and that since you are the boss now you make your own rules. You sent her away; you now have the power to bring her back. It's all about what you want to do. No one can stop you, no? Not eh, Sergio, or Thomas, or Benito or anyone here that works for you." Rosie placed her hands on my shoulder again, reassuring me the decision I made would be the right one.

"Thank you Rosie, I'm going into the study, you should get some rest."

"I will, Nicodemus has a Vet appointment mañana and you know it is awfully difficult to get him to cooperate."

"Good night Rosie."

"Buenas noches Mr. Taliaferro."

I decided to go check in on my first and only love. Once I got into my office I locked the door and pulled up the surveillance cameras. I couldn't watch live time but I could see what she was doing the day before. The feed was 12 hours behind. As I zoomed in on the video of her, there she was. As graceful as she always was, dancing in the garden of her quaint home in the island of St.Thomas. *"She always did love to dance in the flowers."* A tear tried to escape my eye and I fought it back. *"My bella thinks that I don't know what its like to lose someone you love. I know the feeling all too well."*

Paulette

My brain pulsated inside my skull. If this is what an aneurysm felt like, surely I was about to have one. I parted my eyelids slowly; the incandescent hospital light served no assistance to my worsening headache. I watched my darling husband leaneing back uncomfortably in the chair next to my hospital bed.

He's just as handsome as the first day I met him. The fact that he rushed to my side only serves to prove that what we have is real. I simply need to eliminate his distraction. I needed someone to kill Londyn. I reached over to the drawer next to my hospital bed to retrieve my cell phone. I texted Ted:

Me: The bitch has got to go. Can you suggest a good drycleaner?

Ted: I know an excellent drycleaner, good, get the job done right the first time, but they don't come cheap. You want I should set up a meeting?

Me: Yes, make it happen.

When the dust settles and the mayhem clears. I will be the last woman standing. I am his wife, he chose me, and while I may have let myself go, Donald is my husband and she cannot take him away that easily. So simply put, she must die.

Chapter 13

Paulette

It had been two weeks since my meeting with the detective, Donald was being a gem. He waited on me hand and foot. Even in our first years of marriage he had never been this affectionate and doting. But I knew it was fleeting. It was only to bide time and get me back to the place where I didn't ask any questions.

I had already come to the conclusion that the little tramp he was screwing had to go. Once I was released from the hospital I contacted Ted to get the names of the other wives who may or may not know about this little bitch.

I placed a phone call to a man who made it clear he could take care of the problem for one hundred thousand dollars. While we are well off, financially $100k is not something I have readily available. At best I could come up with nearly half. I needed the other wives to cosign and pitch in so that we could get rid of her once and for all. Then our husbands would no longer have her as a distraction. According to Ted's records there were three other homes this Londyn was wrecking without cause or indignation. I knew all three of the women personally. Ericka, wife of Philadelphia

Eagles wide receiver Kelvin Harris, Marisol, wife of Javier Castillo the world renowned cardiac surgeon, and Renee' the wife of the television evangelist David Fonville.

I was a bit apprehensive about how these very different women would react to the news that this one tight ass little slut was attempting to ruin our lives by fucking her way into our men's hearts and wallets! I popped an Ativan to settle my nerves.

"I really must see about getting Botox, I'll call Dr. Aguilar when I finish lunch."

The country club was alive with families and socialites. All of the elite in Philadelphia area belonged and knew each other well, some more than others. I had arranged a small catered lunch with the three ladies in a private dining area in the back of the country club. I figured salmon steaks, fruit sushi, and Bellini's would get these women comfortable enough to share this information with them. I shimmied my rotund behind into the chair at the head of the table and awaited my guests. I had created a separate folder for each one.

Renee who is ever punctual was the first to arrive. Renee is the daughter of James Walker, the real estate tycoon. When he passed she inherited his fortune. So truth be told, her husband's show could be cancelled at any moment and they would still have money until the cows came home.

"Paulette, so sweet of you to have me for lunch! How have you been? We haven't seen each other since the Kentucky Derby in April." We smooched on either side of our faces and she took the seat to my left.

"It has been that long hasn't it! I know Donald and David see each other all the time on the golf course."

"David lives out there! Some Saturdays I won't see that man till 9 or 10 o'clock at night! At least he's not out doing other things." Renee used air quotes when she said "other things." I cleared my throat and took a sip of my bellini. Ericka was next, of the four of us, she is by far the most flashy. Dressed in a leopard print cat suit she strolled in with her Louis Vuitton doggie carrier. In it her pet whom she treats like a child; Buddah. She claims the dog brings her peace. Whatever! Her southern drawl at times is like nails on a chalk board, but she's very sweet.

"Hey ere'body how's y'all doing today?" Ericka removed her ostentatious sunglasses and took the seat to my right.

She sat her doggie carrier on the floor and unzipped it. Out popped the ugliest dog I had ever seen in my life. Ericka grabbed Buddah up and began to lavish him with kisses all over his face. She took her Bellini and poured it into the salad bowl for Buddah to lap up at his leisure.

"My little man just loves his Bellini!"

Renee rolled her eyes. "Are you sure its safe to feed a dog alcohol?"

"Shhh, now Renee honey we don't use the D word. Buddah is just as human as you and I!" She turned to Buddah and began to coddle him. "It's ok baby, Ms. Renee didn't mean it, mommy loves you bb."

I felt a bit of vomit rise in my throat from all the affection she was showing him. I washed it down with another swig of my drink. Twenty minutes flew by and still no sign of Marisol. Just as I was about to call her she came staggering into our section. Clearly intoxicated already, her cigarette dangled dangerously on the edge of her lip. Marisol was a character. If she wasn't drinking then she was putting things up her nose. Strikingly beautiful, she lives a very lonely life. Also barren, she was a victim of female circumcision when she was 12 in her home village. The infection from the improper use of tools caused sterilization.

"Hola muy bonita senoritas. It's a beautiful day, no?"

"Good afternoon Marisol if you'll have a seat I can get this meeting underway."

"Whas dis meetings about anyway?" Marisol's speech slurred a bit as she forced the words from the corners of her mouth. I handed each of them their folders.

"There is no easy way to say this. Upon some investigative work I had done on Donald, the detective I hired uncovered not only was this woman sleeping with my husband but she was sleeping with your husband's as well."

"What in the hell? What type of bull shit is this?" Pain rose up in Ericka's voice, she looked at Buddah to maintain her composure.

"¡Dios mío!" Marisol stood up and stumbled over to the window.

"Dear God, no!" Renee exclaimed as she opened her folder and the first photo was her husband, David, and Londyn in a compromising position. I started to call off the meeting, but I was there for a purpose and I needed to know if these women were on board with me.

"Now ladies, when I tell you what I have in mind, I need it to stay between us. I know someone who can make all of our problems with this little slut go away, but I need your help." I adjusted myself in my seat and looked at each lady to determine who I could and couldn't trust.

"Hell naw, she can't have my husban'. Let me know what we need to do." Ericka pulled out another cigarette and lit the new one off the tip of the last one. She plucked the butt into her glass. Grabbing Buddah off of the table she began to pet him feverishly.

"All husbands cheat amigas, its part of the package. He make sex with her, I make sex with the gardener Hector, and then sometimes we, you know, make sex with each other." Marisol kept her gaze fixed on an object outside the window so we wouldn't see the pain in her eyes. "It's normal to me, and I still get to spend as I like."

Renee stood up and went to try and comfort Marisol.

"Don't you love him?"

"Amor? What in the hell does love have to do with anything? Javier picked me, on a trip to Mexico, we weren't in love, but he offered me something that no man, could offer me. A chance to live well you know? I am not going to be giving that up because some chica is fucking him." She quickly tossed back two more Bellinis and swayed out of the room.

My heart hurt for Marisol and her acceptance of the dysfunctionality of her marriage. But I had bigger fish to fry. I turned my attention back to the two ladies remaning at the table.

"Ladies this little slut is a menace, and she must be dealt with accordingly. I know a man who is willing to assist in taking her out of our hair for a mere 100k."

"Honey a $100k? You know Kelvin is tight with his change, but I have some rainy day funds put up at my momma's house in Birmingham. I will have her send that to me straight away. It may only be $20- or $30k." Ericka blew ring shaped smoke billows into the air above our table.

"Renee what about you?"

Renee rapidly rubbed the 10 carat solitaire that adorned her wedding ring. As if a genie was going to magically appear and grant her a wish to make this all go away. "The bible says, 'thou shalt not kill'."

"I never said anything about killing now did I Renee'? I said he would make her go away, now why would I ask you to be involved in an assassination plot knowing you are the wife of a preacher? What type of woman do you take me for?" For a moment I thought Renee could see through my rouse.

"Well what is he going to do? I doubt it could be anything of the Godly manner."

"Oh chile, please, your man is fucking this trollop and you worried bout if its Godly? You need to be worried about what ungodly things he doin' with her besides kissing her in the car like he doing in that there picture." Ericka extinguished her cigarette on the picture of her husband and Londyn. A small burn hole began to appear and slowly spread.

"Ok, I love my husband and my marriage is of vital importance to me. I can also contribute possibly $25,000 to the removal of this woman from my family's life."

Within a few days the plan was going to be set. Marisol not contributing was going to set me back, but I would come up with something. I was not going to let this whore ruin my life and compromise what I had worked so hard for. My wheels were turning at lightning speed now. I cut into my salmon steak and we ate our lunch in silence.

Chapter 14

Londyn

The warm breeze blew under my skirt and kissed my panty-less ass as I walked to class. Allen tailed close behind as he always did, carrying my books and mumbling to himself about Pythagorean theorems or some shit. I was texting David, he was always so thirsty for time and attention, never really sex, and he just wanted someone to talk dirty with because his wife was so uptight. Mid-text I ran straight into a set of washboard abs.

"Excuse you." I looked up at the man towering over me.His smile was like sunshine, and his eyes were the same color as my Tiffany's boxes. Damn he was sexy.

"G'day! Why aren't you a dashing Sheila?" He smiled again and his skin glistened.

"Umm, for one, my name is Londyn, two, you're in my way." I pushed past him, determined to make it to class on time.

Allen steadily eyed the handsome stranger.

"My apologies filly, I be Vincent, here on exchange from the great state of Sydney!" He turned to Allen and extended his hand. "Hey there bastard, I like your goggies."

"I'm sorry sir, but I won't stand for any derogatory references made in my direction. You may address me as Allen."

"Have you done any recent television work? Your face is strikingly familiar to me." Allen furrowed his brow and reluctantly shook Vincent's hand in return. "Well Vince, gotta go, maybe I'll see you around, maybe I won't. Later!"

"Ah…don't step off so quickly doll. Might I toss back a little grogg and some Barbie[2] with you tonight?"

"Uhh, ok whatever that means. I guess. Take my number. Call me later." My pussy was dripping wet at the thought of this tall handsome stranger from Sydney, wherever the hell that is, wanting to take me out. I was definitely going to have fun climbing up and down his tall ass.

"Allen, where in the hell is Sydney?" He still had a puzzled look on his face as if he was trying to recollect where he had seen Vincent before.

"Sydney is the capital of Australia, the smallest continent in the world, once owned by England, Sydney's current population is 2.5 million. Major exports are fishing and textiles. Run by High Chancellor Roberts, the island was once used as a prison for English men." Allen rambled off in one breath as if he recalled it from some database inside his mind. "I'm not sure about him my auspicious amiga, I know I've seen him before. I never forget a face."

"Come off it Allen, that six degrees of separation is bull shit. Enough with the conspiracy theories for the

_____

[2] Australian Barbeque

day ok?" Allen could be so annoying when the tiny hamster wheels inside his mind began to turn feverishly.

"Mark my words my beloved, raven-haired beauty. I will recall where I've seen him and bring it to the forefront of my memory in one of our next conversations, which I covet so dearly."

"Ok, Allen whatever you say. Can we please get to class,

goodness, you know this whole school thing is new for me."

"As you wish, angelic one. I think you may be the matriarch of my revitalization." Allen swiftly grabbed my hand and kissed it. I felt a little embarrassed by his odd display of affection.

"Allen, please just call me Londyn. That other shit is weird." He opened the door to the classroom for me and we slipped inside just in time to grab a decent seat. I couldn't get Vincent's smile and the blueness of his eyes off my mind. Yea next chance I get, I'm going to fuck him silly. Never had Australian dick.

***

As I was leaving class I got a text from the dean, I hadn't really had much to say to him lately. Especially since I actually had to do my school work, I don't fuck

95

for free, and truthfully I wasn't getting anything out of the deal. I crossed campus to his office quickly. I didn't really feel like arguing with him today. I smiled at the thought of running into Blue Eyes again as I was making my way to the Dean's office. Once inside the office he began to shower me with kisses. I turned my head and rejected his advances.

"Baby girl what's wrong? You haven't been calling me, or coming to see me like you used to. I know I was busy there for a bit taking care of my wife but that's all taken care of now."

"I just really don't have time. See initially our agreement was I fuck you when and how you wanted it, and I would get passing grades without doing anything. You would get to keep my daddy's money and I would get to keep my free time. However that doesn't seem to be what's going on."

"Londyn, darling it's not that simple." He attempted to reach out and touch my face.

"No, see DONALD; it is that simple, I don't fuck for free. It's a waste of time. You've gotten all the free pussy you are going to get, and let's be real, you can't afford my lifestyle. After all, you drive a used Porsche!"

"Please, can we work something out?" Donald got on his knees and tried to put his head under my skirt. He cupped my ass with both of his hands and pulled me into his mouth. The rush of heat to my pussy nearly knocked me off balance.

"Stop, please..." My words were quickly enclosed in my moans. There pinned against the door, I came to a shocking realization. The only difference between me and a common whore were the quality of the panties we wore. And I didn't have any on.

Paulette

Donald was back to his regular self, being distant, barely touching me, and ignoring me daily. Ericka had given me a catalog to Pure Romance, for me to acquire some tools for my own self pleasure. However, masturbation had never quite done the trick for me.

"If he can find someone to fuck his brains out so can I."

Mr. Zonkers was stretched out across the bay window basking in the fall afternoon sunshine. I stroked his belly a bit and he purred lovingly. I grabbed a Diet Pepsi from our kitchen and took a seat in the den. I really wanted to hire someone to fuck me silly, but it had to be quick, precise, and discreet. I contemplated calling Hector, our gardener, but he didn't turn me on. He had the overall look I like in a Latino man, but he was dumb as a bag of rocks.

"Who can I call?" As if the infidelity gods were smiling upon my poor, dismal sex life, I distinctly remembered Marisol mumbling about hiring a man to "fuck her sideways," as she put.

As quick as my chubby fingers could dial Marisol's number she was on the line.

"Hola mi amiga, como esta?"

"Hey Marisol, it's Paulette, I wanted to ask you something if you have a moment."

"Sure sure, anything for you chica, what choo wan?"

"Eh...Um... I'm not sure how to ask you this." I wrung my hands tightly and took a massive gulp of my Diet Pepsi. I was hoping the sting of the carbonation would help me find my words a little easier.
"Ah chica, we are friends, just spit it out!" Marisol laughed, when she wasn't drunk she was jovial, sometimes she was both drunk and jovial. Maybe it was her anti-psych meds.

"Well you know Donald and I are having some issues. I was wondering if you could refer me to a gentleman to help me handle some of my needs." I felt as if the two ton brick that was resting on my protruding mass of a belly had been lifted.

"Wha? What choo want girl, someone come fuck you brains out? I can arrange that. Julio don't come cheap you know but he will handle his business."

"The cost is irrelevant. How soon can he be over here?"

"I say give him about an hour, chica. He's all the way in Chester."

"Ok. Should I give you my address or will you have him call me?"

"I just have him call you. Trust me you're gonna get your pesos worth."

"Ok thank you." A very Cheshire like smile formed as I hung up the phone. I went to shower and change for my session with Julio. *"Two wrongs don't make it right, but we will for damn sure be even. And once she's out of the picture everything will be just fine."*

Chapter 16

Giuseppe

I stepped out into the night breeze. I walked quickly and with purpose from my office to my car. I had given my driver the evening off as I had pressing business to attend to.

I turned my cell phone off as I crossed into New Jersey. I didn't want to be disturbed where I was going. My mind raced at the thought of the information I was about to receive. Pulling up to Si'Sicily the restaurant was dark. *"Great."* Just as I was about to get back into my car and head home, Yono, one of

Carmelengo's protégé's came around to the front of the building from a secluded alleyway.

"Don Talliaferro, this way please."

The back entrance to the restaurant was dank, reeking of day's old garbage and cat piss. I ducked as I crossed the entryway.

Scoda was seated at a small table and Carmelengo was to his left.

The looks on their faces let me know this was more than an average business call.

"Salutare." I hugged and greeted both of these highly respected men.

"I wish I was coming to you today under better circumstances Giuseppe. You are like a son to me. If anything I would never want to see you hurt."

"Sal, you helped raise me as I was raising my daughter. You are the reason my organization runs as quietly and as undetected as it does. For that I am eternally grateful." Yono passed me a stogie. I slowly inhaled its rich aroma. Mixes of bourbon, chestnut, and thyme could be smelled as I clipped the end and lit the cigar. The rich aroma swirled around our meeting of the minds like a moat does a castle. The information being passed along was the drawbridge to entry.

"You asked we should find out who did the kid your daughter was seeing. Through a little leg work, and some arm twisting we got the name. This is not easy though Giuseppe.

Under normal circumstances we would have handled the fuck and had his head here on ice waiting for you. However, this is one we both feel as though you must personally handle yourself."

I felt a tightness growing in my chest. What or who was so important or high ranking that they couldn't personally deliver his or her head to me on a platter? What were they going to tell me?

"Just tell me Carmelengo. I am not the same boy who chased chickens in Sicily. I can handle it."

Scoda interjected. "How loyal is your boy Sergio?"

"Sergio? He's a loose cannon sometimes but he's always represented my organization well."

"He's Rosa's boy right?" Carmelengo rubbed his chin in a worrying manner.

"Yes, Sergio is Rosa's son."

"Does he have a thing for your Bella?" Scoda pushed back from the table and folded his aging hands in his lap.

"He is very protective of her. As he should be, he is my second in command. He wants what is best for her." The words came out of my mouth in slow motion. As soon as I let them slip I wanted to reach into the atmosphere and pull them back. Here it had been right under my nose the entire time. Sergio had killed Jordan. I unknowingly had my daughter's boyfriend's killer under my nose the entire time and failed to see the signs. *"How could I be so stupid?"* My mind raced. I got up from the table, no more words between me and these men needed to be spoken. An eye for an eye is how we do things in our world. Loyalty is everything. Sergio had broken the number one code, and for it he would pay. With his life.

***

"Thomas, listen very carefully to me. I need Sergio taken to the place we took that guy that time. Just me and him. Set it up I will take care of the rest."

"Rope or chains?" Thomas understood what needed to be done without much being said. He wasn't the type to ask many questions.

"Rope. I will be there in an hour."

"It will be done." Thomas hung up and I lit my second cigar of the evening. Chain smoking wouldn't ease the anger that was boiling up inside me right now. It took a little over an hour to get to the warehouse where I instructed Thomas to bring Sergio. It was in a deserted part of Exton, where the "family" owned most of the properties. It was rare I ever had any personal ties to incidences of this caliber. However Sergio had committed a reprehensible offense. The cuff of my bone white suit pants kissed the ground as the gravel underneath my feet was dispersed as evenly as my unwavering footsteps. When I entered the warehouse

Sergio's rustlings echoed into the emptiness of the building. A few more steps through the building and I saw him; tied at his hands and his feet, suspended at least six feet into the air. The rope holding him between the here and now was a few feet away from me on my left hand side. Below him awaited a fiery death. A shipping barrel; ignited and begging him to be dropped in. The flames licked and kissed the edges of the barrel as he tried his hardest to keep his feet from meeting the fire. Thomas had really worked him over, his eyes were nearly swollen shut. All I could do was shake my head. I couldn't believe Sergio had gotten so power hungry.

"Sergio. You were like a fratellino[3] to me. I trusted you with my life. With my family. Most of all with my Bella. You made moves without my consent and that shows disloyalty. I am going to ask you a question. I expect an honest answer." I grabbed my third cigar of the night out of my suit jacket and lit it. The flames from my lighter seemed to call to the flames dancing in the barrel. I blew o-ring shaped smoke billows into the air as I walked around Sergio. I pulled on the rope to test its strength, it tightened on both his wrists and ankles, he screamed but the gag in his mouth swallowed his failed attempt to cry out. "Oh, I'm sorry did that hurt?" I walked back near the entrance and grabbed a chair. Seated directly in front of the barrel, I was Pontius Pilot and I was certainly going to crucify this fuck face for his crimes against my family.

---

[3] Brother

"Mi hai tradito. Come osi disrepect la mia famiglia, e la mia organizzazione[4]. One question only. Did you kill Jordan?"

He rapidly shook his head from left to right; his eyes wrought with fear. I knew it was only in an attempt to save his sorry ass.

"Ever been this close to death Sergio?" I stared at him for a while, at this boy turned man who I had practically raised along with myself, watched him rise through the ranks of my organization and gain my trust. While we are all natural born killers by way of bloodline, most kill, or maim with intention. I'm quite sure he assumed in killing Jordan that he was vindicating my family and my organization, but he couldn't have been more wrong. My daughter, Londyn is my most prized possession, my crowning achievement and while she may not have chosen who I wanted her to be with she genuinely loved that boy. I would never in a million years do to my daughter what my parents did to me and Rebecca. I looked up from my deep train of thought; the hell fire was waiting for its victim elect, it had burned without him long enough.

---

[4] This is tradition. Not only did he disrespect my family but also my organization.

"Sergio, you could have come to me instead of taking matters into your own hands. You aren't a boss, and now because of one irrational decision you won't ever get to be one. See, I could easily sit here all night watching you suffer, watching the metal on the wing tip shoes I got you burn to the point where you plead for me to take your shoes off, but then the fire will get a taste of your flesh. But I'm not in the mood for that today.

Occhio per occhio Sergio. È figlio di unacagna.[5]" I tossed my partially smoked, still smoldering cigar into the barrel, the flames

rose up immediately. I released the rope from its anchor. Sergio had been tried by fire and proven guilty. There would be no resurrection for him. The distinct sound of flesh burning away from muscle and bone is indescribable. As I turned my back to exit the warehouse, he writhed in agony as his clothes turned to ash and the top layer of his epidermis melted away like salt water taffy on a blazing summer afternoon. Once outside the cool night air filled my lungs and renewed my spirit. I looked down at the cuff of my pants leg and noticed some ashen marks. *"Damn this suit has got to go to the cleaners."*

***

Back at home I parked and made a bee line for my office. Thomas was seated on the couch, nursing his swollen knuckles. I poured us each a glass of scotch on the rocks. Each sip we took in silence spoke volumes. Though Thomas isn't an official member of my organization, I trust him with my life, and the life of my daughter long before any of these Wop's. Thomas

---

[5] An eye for an eye Sergio. Loyalty is everything.

and his family have worked for my family for over 30 years. We were raised together, his mother and father both worked for my parents. He is my confidant, my safe deposit box, my fisticuffs if needed, and the best damn shot on this side of the Hudson.

"Tomorrow," Thomas said flatly without looking up from his diminishing glass of alcohol.

"Tomorrow then," I downed the rest of my glass, and rose to head up to bed.

Chapter 16

Londyn

I was in school early, half attempting to earn some gym credit, half attempting to get a little attention while dripping with sweat. My legs pushed through the burn my muscles were experiencing as the treadmill I had been holding hostage for an hour ramped up to 6.3. My breasts bounced wildly as I was determined to shave off as many calories as humanly possible in one day. Gym Class Heroes rocked out on my Pandora radio. The heavy bass bumped in my Blueooth earphones. I looked as if I had participated in a wet T-shirt contest;my tank was completely soaked. I pulled it off over my head and kept my stride. I looked to my left and nearly fell off. Vincent was standing there flashing his mesmerizing million dollar smile my way.

"Good day, beautiful lady."

A wave of nervousness washed over me. "Hi." I pretended that my pussy didn't throb when I heard his voice.

"Now why are you in here running a marathon lady?"

I grabbed my towel and took a few sips of my Fiji water. I hit the stop button on the treadmill and hopped off. "I like to stay in shape, normally I would just fuck somebody but that's getting kind of old." *"Oh my God did I just say that? What the fuck is he going to think?"*

"Lady, you have got one awesome sense of humor!" He smiled and I creamed a little in my pants. I was still trying to play it cool. I hadn't been this way around a guy since, since Jordan.

"You have got to let me take you out."

"How are you going to take me out and you are the foreigner? Do you know your way around the city? It's my birthday Saturday, how about I have my driver pick you up and we can go out. You'll pay of course." He grabbed my hand and placed his perfectly sun-kissed lips on it. He lingered for a bit, then his amazingly ocean blue eyes locked with mine.

"I'd be more than honored to escort you on your birthday! Of course I'll pay, I wouldn't dream of it any other way. You do like McDonald's right?"

"Now who's a comedian. Text me your address." I grabbed his Blackberry world phone and began imputing my number in it.

"Don't forget the +011 before your number." He was running his fingers through my hair as I stored my number in his phone and he texted me his address.

I was smiling from ear to ear as I walked away from the man I was sure was going to give me the best birthday sex of my life. Allen must have been watching us from across the gym; as soon as I walked away from Vincent he joined me in stride.

"Why good morning most illustrious Londyn," He adjusted his glasses and pulled the rubber band tighter on his dreads. When Allen wasn't being extremely weird he was actually kind of sexy.

"Hey Vi, I mean Allen, what's up?"

"So you are that caught up in the conundrum that is VINCENT that you would refer to me as such?"

"It was a mistake Allen so- not that serious. Relax!" I grabbed him around his waist lightly and he blushed.

"All is forgiven my dubious darling. What will we be doing to celebrate the day of your birth? Some big soiree I'm sure."

"Actually no, this will be my first birthday in two years without Jordan. It's not the same. I'm going to go to dinner with Vincent, and maybe catch a show. I'm sure my dad would like that. A nice quite calm celebration."

"How mature of you dearest Londyn, is this a private dinner? Might I tag along, don't worry I won't bring anyone unworthy of your presence."

"Oh Allen, I'm sorry it's just going to be a date with me and Vincent. He's so sexy! I'm excited. You and I can do something next week, I promise." Allen's face fell. All the hope he had that he would finally get to spend some special time with me had been dashed in one fell swoop by this hot and sexy thunder from down under.

"No problem, my beautiful butterfly. I can't pinpoint where I know that guy from. His face is too familiar, I'll figure it out. Alas dear princess I will have a gift for you, I am making something."

"Oh, thank you so much Allen I'm sure whatever you get me I will love. Let's get to class." Allen held the door for me as he always does, and we headed out of the gymnasium and across campus to our first class of the day.

Paulette

Summer raindrops ran in between my toes as I walked hurriedly to the spot where I was to meet the "Drycleaner". He demanded half up front to take care of my problem. Well not just my problem, this little bitch is a problem for anyone who has a happy home. Real or imagined. Since Marisol backed out I sold our party boat to make up the difference, $50,000 in small un-marked bills is what he requested. He wanted to meet at the park across from the University where Donald works.

Initially I was nervous, thinking what if my husband saw me. But then I thought about it, who cares if he sees me with another man, that may make him step his game up. The drycleaner requested I sit at the bench next to the fountain. So me and my leopard spotted umbrella took our seat and waited. With each man that walked past my heart beat quickened wondering if he was the one. First a beautiful brown man with a Great Dane and the best set of legs I had seen in years walked past. He looked at me, smiled and kept right along on his walk. Next a portly man, such as myself, took a seat on the same bench as me. My mind raced with anticipation.

"Good Morning sir, how about those Red Sox?" I nervously let the words fall out of my mouth.

"Lady I don't know what planet you're from, but this is Philadelphia. Eagles and Phillies country. Who gives a damn about the Red Sox?" As if the words Red Sox had offended him greatly, he scoffed at me and got up off of the bench.

"Where is he?" I mumbled under the halo of my umbrella. I rested one hand on my muffin top and contemplated leaving. "He has 5 more minutes or I'm leaving to go get a cheesesteak." As if he read my mind, my phone started to ring.

"Hello?...Yes I'm here waiting for you...Ok I will place it in the trash can...ok....ok. Thank you." I placed the black book bag inside of the trash can next to the bench. I began to walk away. I turned back for a second and noticed a tall black man with dreads had taken my seat on the bench. *That has got to be him!"* He was a bit unlike what I would imagine in the man who would be handling this type of business for me. He looked more like a reject from Marilyn Manson's summer camp. I didn't want to stare too long for fear of blowing the deal. IfI could identify him, or whatever the reasons are people kill people who can pick them out of a line up. I turned around once more and dread head looked to be surfing the internet on his laptop. *"Who uses their laptop outside in the rain? Yea he's got to be the one."*

Chapter 17

Allen

In the most prestigious and calculating manner possible I crafted a creation only fit for a queen. I made Londyn a sculpture, a small scale model of the city in which she got her namesake and of the Egyptian Goddess, Isis, which her aura and presence remind me most of. I have been slaving over this project for a few weeks now. I couldn't quite decide what to give a woman who has the universe at her fingertips. Money is no object for this precious pearl, I had to bestow upon her something both unique and thoughtful. Packing her gifts safely in the under carriage of my scooter I sojourned to the Taliaferro estate. *"What a tremendous abode to have grown up within."* The stately family butler, Thomas, gave me entrance to the home. I was awestruck at the architectural detailing. The vaulted ceilings in the foyer rivaled even the most famed structure. Londyn was sun-bathing alongside the pool in all her glory when I took a seat beside her. Her beauty rendered me speechless. Her skin was the color of fresh honey, as smooth as the rarest Egyptian silk, she was perfect. Never a hair out of place she was the epitome of excellence in my eyes. If I carved her likeness out of the finest imported granite it still would certainly not do her any justice.

"Born day salutations to you my queen." I dropped to one knee and held out a single solitary Anonmea for her. Londyn looked over and smiled briefly.

"Thank you Allen. This flower is pretty. I would invite you to take a dip in the pool but I was just about to go get dressed."

"My dearest angel on earth, this flower is but the first of three celebratory gifts I have for you. Might we briefly retire to your quarters so that I may bestow these gifts upon you? I promise not to keep you from your errands long."

"Come on Allen, I don't want to sound ungrateful but I have shit to do and you just came unannounced." Londyn's hips bent and swayed in the summer breeze. Surely she must be of the bloodline of the Sirens of Sirenia because any man who would gaze upon her hips would be mesmerized. Once inside the adjacent pool house, I took a seat on her chaise loungue. I removed the gifts from their protective cases and set them on the table in front of me. Londyn had gone upstairs to get dressed. My heart quickened with excitement when I heard her footsteps headed back down the steps. I met her at the steps and led her into the living room where her gifts awaited her.

"Allen what are these?"

Quite impressed with myself I picked up the Isis first and handed to it her. "The goddess Isis (the mother of Horus) was the first daughter of Geb, god of the Earth, and Nut, the goddess of the Overarching Sky, and was born on the fourth intercalary day. At some time Isis and Hathor had the same headdress. In later myths about Isis, she had a brother, Osiris, who became her husband, and she then was said to have conceived Horus. Isis was instrumental in the resurrection of Osiris when he was murdered by Set.

Her magical skills restored his body to life after she gathered the body parts that had been strewn about the earth by Set.] This myth became very important in later Egyptian religious beliefs... She reminded me most of you." I had rambled that all off like someone had pressed play on the encyclopedia section of my frontal lobe.

"Ok, I have no idea what any of that meant but thank you and what is this other thing?"

"It's a replica of the city in which your name is derived from. London for Londyn."

"Aww, that's sweet thank you Allen, I'm not sure what I'm going to do with a small city, but I appreciate it, thank you. I will call you later, I have to go find something to wear for tonight."

"Oh of course, birthday celebrations, a meal and libations perhaps? Might I join you and your crew of lovely ladies?"

"Umm, Allen I'm going on a date with Vincent. Otherwise I would invite you, but I really like him and this is going to be our first date! He's so special."

My blood began to boil beneath my skin. The feelings I had about this exchange student were not positive in nature. He is certainly a most dubious foe, and I will not rest until I have this conundrum figured out.

Londyn

Sure, I appreciated the gifts Allen gave me but, truth be told, who knew what the hell they were or what his odd ass reasoning was behind it. Later for that shit, it was surely going to make my head hurt trying to figure it all out. I needed to grab an outfit for my date with

Vincent. He was surely fuckable, and if anyone was worthy of this soon to be 22 ass it was him. Hell, I was dying to see what some real foreign dick was about anyway. Running late to meet Corynne in King of Prussia, I quickly left the house and hit the expressway. A new Louis and some Loubies will be the perfect complement to the La Perla panties and whatever dress I find. Plus there's nothing better than the way my legs look in the air in 5 inch red bottomed stilettos. The plan was to use daddy's driver, pick up Vincent, grab dinner, and then meet up with Cory and my other girls at the club and party until I can't remember. But I can certainly imagine waking up with Vincent in my bed and every hole on my body aching so good!

Traffic was light for a Saturday afternoon on the Schuykill I got to King of Prussia quickly and hit Corynne up to see where she was at in the mall. Of course she was in Neiman Marcus ogling over the fresh shipment of Jeffery Campbell shoes.

"Do you see these? Do you fucking see these?" Corynne sung in her most chipper shopping voice.

"Hey love, what's up?" We air kissed and she handed me a shoe off of the display. The reps in the shoe department knew us well. No need to ask us what sizes we needed, they already knew.

"These are to die for Londyn! I can't take it, I need them all!"

"I am so agreeing with you right now, what am I going to wear tonight?"

"Girl whatever you wear I'm sure you will be thebomb.com! Oh yea Javier wanted to know if we needed bottle service tonight, for when we get to the club. He has a friend I need you to meet, can you say the Cape of Spain in 2 weeks!" Corynne held her hand up for a high five, and it went unreturned.

I'm bringing Vincent tonight; I don't think that would be a good look to have Javier and his friend all on my back and I'm bringing a date." I signaled the shoe girl, who's skin could use a serious micro-dermabrasion and some proactive or something. She scurried to the back bringing out not only the Louboutins but also the Jefferey Campbells and a few other styles.

"Wait you are bringing the exchange student out to party for your birthday? Does he have money; is he like the son of the king of Australia?" Corynne's tone was so beyond over the conversation we were having. As she paraded back and forth in front of the mirror kicking her left leg up and practicing poses for her impromptu photo shoot with the paparazzi later tonight.

"Cory please, to tell you the truth he's the first man I've seen since Jordan that I actually wanted to fuck. There is something about him. Most dudes I see I'm not even attracted to, it's all about what they can do for me."

"Ok and what the fuck is wrong with that again? I swear Lon, since you started this school shit you're starting to act like you actually give a fuck about people. I mean after the whole thing with the grunge boy in the library,"

"You mean the bookstore?"

"Bitch, you knew what the fuck I meant! Like since when did you give a fuck about whether I called it a bookstore or a God Damn library? Get your life together, we are too rich and sex is too easy to get from men with money to fuck some exchange student for free." Corynne had bad skin girl carry her mountain of selections up to the register so she could check out. "Ms. Diaz your total is $11,425.67, how will you be taking care of this today?"

Corynne swiftly slid one of her suitor's black American Express card across the counter to take care of the hefty tab she had run up.

I grabbed a sexy pair of python Louboutins and we rushed off to find killer dresses for the night. As we hit the escalator, my phone started jumping in my pocket. I pulled it out and glanced to see who it was.

"Damn, I do not feel like talking to him!"

"Who?"

"Donald. He's such a pussy."

"No, you're the pussy, you're the one who was supposed to be fucking him in exchange for not having to do school work and look here your dumb ass is with a wet ass and still studying!" Corynne burst into a fit of giggles and skipped up the escalator.

I sent Donald to voicemail and wondered if Corynne was right. Did I get suckered into giving up sex to the Dean of Students and now here I am studying my ass off to get good grades?

Chapter 18

Giuseppe

The sun was barely setting behind the mountains that landscaped the countryside when I stormed into the pool house. Londyn had her day's purchases spread out on her chaise marveling at all of them. When I burst through the door she hopped to her feet.

"Hey daddy! Happy birthday to me! Look at all the stuff you got me!"

"Cut the shit, Londyn." The excitement in her eyes waned, clearly she knew I was pissed.

"Dang, what now daddy?" She started to organize her purchases to busy herself while I reamed her a new asshole. "Who in the fuck gave you the authority to acquisition my car service, birthday or not?"

"Umm, daddy since when can't I take the car service wherever I needed to go? Be lucky that I'm not going to drive and possibly total the Maserati tonight!" Londyn stood a stone's throw away from me, arms crossed and scowling like a toddler who was told they couldn't have the last cookie.

"Why are you taking the car service to the Extended Stay? What could possibly be there that has to do with the celebration of your birthday?"

"I'm picking up a friend daddy, goodness gracious not everyone has mansions to live in." The sparkle in her eye let me know she was full of shit.

"Who is he?" My chest swelled with frustration. I never raised my daughter to be a whore and this phase she was going through was going to give me a coronary I was certain of it.

"Daddy, I really don't have to tell you the names of all my birthday celebration guests. Get over yourself." Londyn ducked through a space between me and the corner I was trying to back her into. "Everything isn't for everybody Giuseppe."

I gave up, threw my hands up and made my way towards the door. "Let's hope your ass doesn't end up on page six again. You will learn the value of public transportation quickly if you do." I left her standing there jaw wide open at the mere mention of me taking her car and revoking her access to my car services. I retired to my office to let a double shot of Jack ease my mind.

Londyn

I swear my dad is so extra! I really don't understand what the problem is with the whole car service thing. Seriously I'm not going to fuck Vincent in the back of the limousine; unless that is what he is into. Upstairs in my room I pulled my brand new Carmelita Couture flashing yellow bandeu dress out of its garment bag and slipped it on. No bra or panties required when you plan on being naked by the end of the night. The python skin Louboutin's made my already long legs look even more sexy. *"Someone is going to get a crotch shot pic tonight,"* I said to myself smiling. I stepped out of the five inch cfmp's and ran down my steps to let my makeup artist, Charese, in. This woman could totally make any ugly girl pretty, makeup does wonders for horse-faced bitches. So when she already has a beautiful canvas to work with? Watch the fuck out! I always end up looking like I should be on the cover of Vogue Italy or some shit, seriously.

"Hey girl!" Charese chirped in her always pleasant voice. She may be the only woman I know who owns more Louie than me. Clad in a Dior tee and a banging pair of True Religion jeans she was the effortlessly casual chic girls see in the mall and instantly want to match her fly. Her Caesar had me almost wanting to pull an Amber Rose, but I love my long hair too much!

"Are you coming out with us tonight?" We walked back upstairs to my vanity. It was the room with the best lighting for make-up. I pulled two crisp $50.'s from my wallet and handed them to her before taking my seat in my vanity chair.

"Girl no, I'd love to, but I didn't get a haircut so I don't have that to do! Plus I have a date with Marcus!"

"Marcus?" I looked up at her as she applied primer to my face. "Who the fuck is Marcus?"

"The bottle of wine that's waiting on me when I get my ass in the house!" We both laughed.

"Girl you are the most!" She finished up my face, and I sent her on her way. Then with shoes in hand I hurried to the main house to meet our driver out front. My driver for the evening was Paul, a balding black man whose sweet disposition always made me smile.

"Hey Ms. Londyn, happy early birthday! Where are we off to this evening?"

"Well I need to pick my friend up first then Thomas made us reservations at Fogo De Chao on Chesnut."

"Excellent choice pretty lady." I handed Paul the address to the hotel where Vincent was staying while here on exchange. I called his phone and shortly after he emerged from the hotel looking better than the first time I had ever laid eyes on him.

It seemed he could clean up really well. His eyes sparkled in the light of the setting sun, and I was ready to blow off the whole evening and run back up to his hotel room with him. He slid into the limousine and nearly sat in my lap, my heart started racing at the anticipation of him touching me. His Ken-blonde hair was perfectly trimmed and his nails were freshly manicured. *"I wonder if he shaves?"* I shook my head and shifted myself in my seat. I prayed my wetness wouldn't transfer onto my dress as we rode back into downtown Philadelphia. We rode in basic silence, I was so nervous for some reason. When we pulled up in front of the restaurant, Vincent hopped out before Paul could to open my door. As he helped me out of the car he pulled me close to him and tried to stare through me.

"Happy birthday my lady. Awful glad you chose to spend it with me."

I could feel his heart nearly beating out of his chest with anticipation. I craned my neck and planted a soft sensual kiss on his left cheek. Through the large Grecian style doors into the restaurant we walked hand in hand. A stunning amazon like woman greeted us at the door.

"Welcome to Fogo De Chao. Do you have a reservation?"

I rolled my eyes impatiently. I hated it when I went into an establishment and they didn't already know who I was.

"Taliaferro, private party of two."

Amazon woman immediately changed her disposition, even seemed to stand up more straight. "Oh Ms. Taliaferro it is such a pleasure to have you, allow me to show you to your dining area. The richness of the burgundy melted into the walls of our private dining room. Reserve bottles lined the far corner, and the dimness of the candles made Vincent's eyes dance in the light. As we dined and sipped imported Brazilian merlot Vincent finally struck up a conversation.

"So my beautiful birthday lady, no birthday would be complete without a gift. I know that I haven't known you long, however just being in your presence excites me. I am dying to know why a shelia like yourself hasn't been collared by anyone yet."

Not feeling up to crying on my birthday, I looked at him from behind the rim of my wine glass. "I haven't been collared as you call it because I don't want to be. Love left me a little under 6 months ago." Sensing that it was something I didn't want to talk about Vincent reached into his pocket and pulled out a small box with a hot pink bow and slid it across the table to me without uttering a word.

"What's this?" Vincent was still silent, just smiling pleased with himself. Inside the small box was a blue diamond tennis bracelet. It was the same unique color blue as my grandmother's necklace that hung from my neck at this very moment. I fanned my face so the tears I was fighting back wouldn't ruin my $100.00 makeup job. Vincent got up from the table walked over and kissed me. His lips lingered on mine, not really wanting to let go. I shivered from head to toe as he caressed the side of my face. There is just something amazing about this man. I can't put my finger on it.

" The first time I laid eyes on you, I noticed the necklace you wear around your neck. I half figured it had to have some sort of sentimental value being that you never take it off. So I used my bit of cash to find a bracelet that you would never want to take off either."

"Oh Vincent that is so sweet, but we barely know each other, and I know Im really awesome but you didn't have to do this."

"I like you Ms.Londyn, you are the prettiest girl I think I have ever seen. Are you ready to skip this place and have some real birthday fun?" Vincent rubbed his hands together like he had a plan.

"Trust me, NO ONE knows how to party like me! Let's go!" I stood up and realized I was tipsy. I stumbled a bit and he helped me regain my balance.

Vincent kept his hand at the base of my spine to steady my walk as we exited the restaurant. The cool night air had my nipples standing at attention as we waited a few moments for Paul to arrive in the front of the restaurant. Out of the corner of my eye I could have sworn I saw Allen charging at us. His eyes wild with fear he pushed Vincent away from me.

"You are no exchange student sir you stay away from her. I know exactly who you are. It took me quite some time to figure it out but you stay away." Vincent stumbled back and rebounded certainly ready to defend himself if Allen would swing on him.

"Allen, what the fuck are you doing? It's my birthday! How did you know I was here?"

"Londyn, my beautiful flower, please forgive me for ruining any festivities you were partaking in. However this man is not who he says he is. When you updated your Facebook with your location I had to come down here to let you know myself." I grabbed Vincent's hand and the line in the sand was drawn.

"Allen look, I put up with your OCD, your over use of large words and strange gifts but I will not let you attack this man on my birthday and he did nothing wrong. So just stay away. If you want to even consider still being my friend you will leave now."

"But rosebud he's not who he says he is, he's dangerous. "

"I'm sure he couldn't be any more dangerous than spending an afternoon with you. I could have certainly died of a coronary a few times. Allen fucking leave, seriously. You're blowing my high." I pulled Vincent's hand to let him know that the conversation was done. Allen's face lay in a million pieces around his feet. The dismay was evident on his face. "But, Londyn…"

"But what, Allen? Leave me the FUCK ALONE!" Vincent sensed my frustration and interjected in the conversation.

"Look buddy, the lady doesn't want to be bothered on her birthday. Let's not make this more difficult than it has to be." He gripped Allen's shoulder to let him know in so many words that he could break him in half if he applied just the tiniest bit more pressure. Allen hung his head and sauntered off. I slid into the back of the limo and quickly flipped my shoes off. I placed my feet in Vincent's lap and he rubbed them intently. I sipped Moet from the bottle; as I let the bubbles in the liquid-courage erase the embarrassing scene from the minutes before. Vincent grabbed my right foot and began to kiss it softly, my pussy was panting with excitement. He ran his hands up and down my thighs. I took my left foot and rubbed it across the growing bulge in his pants. I kicked my foot from his grasp and sat up to straddle him, I kissed and licked his neck and collar bone hoping he would fuck me mindless in the back of the limo on the way to meet Corynne at the club. He pulled my dress down slightly in the front and swallowed my breast into his mouth. I wanted him inside me so bad. *"Fuck it. I'm on some hoe shit. It's my birthday and I want dick,"* I thought to myself as I attempted to unfasten his belt to take what I wanted. Vincent's arms became stiff, he pulled my dress back up and lifted my face to his.

"Not like this darling."

"Why not? Shit, it's my birthday." I started to pout but the sensation of his fingers running up and down my back stopped it dead in its tracks.

"Baby when searching forever too many people push for the right now. This is right now and you deserve better then to be hopped on in the back of a moving vehicle on our way to a party."

He lifted me off of him and adjusted his erection. I felt like more of a slut than ever, here this man was paying attention to me, listening to me and wanted to take time to get to know me and all I could think about was how good his dick would feel inside me. He kissed me on my forehead and looked at me with eyes that could go on forever. I rested on his chest and I felt safe for the first time in five months.

Chapter 19

Londyn

It had been three weeks since my birthday and fall was in full swing. I was enjoying not only my full class schedule but all of the time I was spending with Vincent. We spent time with each other every day. The craziest thing was that he wouldn't fuck me. He had come out to the pool house; even stayed the night but he would hold me until I drifted off and then go down stairs and get on the couch. It was really fucking with me, but if I didn't know better I'd say he was trying to get me to fall in love with him. Between school and him I had barely any time for the married men I was entertaining before. Plus that was getting boring, I'd much rather spend time staring into Vincent's eyes. His touch was like a shock wave, it sent ripples through my body. I was so open off of the energy he gave me. Allen avoided us at any interval, he no longer sat next to me in class and when I walked by he hung his head. In our regular Monday morning class I was seated in my standard seat, regretting wearing jeans so tight you could see my thong imprint. *"What the fuck was I thinking?"* Mr. Fountain looked up from his water bottle that obviously held a few shots of vodka along with whatever else.

"Ms. Taliaferro, the dean needs to see you in his office please."

"What could Donald possibly want now?"

"Excuse me?"

"Nothing, I'll be back. This is some high school shit, going to the principal's office. What the fuck." I grabbed my netbook, Tory Burch bag and folder and stomped out of the class room.

"Wait till I get in here with Donald's ass, like really bitch you gonna call me in the fucking office like I'm a little kid?"

I walked into his office, past the students waiting in the lobby, and his nosey ass secretary. I flung his office door open and there was a tiny little Indian boy talking about why he needed more college classes.

"Excuse me Habib, Akbar or whatever your name is, I really could care less about what you're talking about, but I'm about to flip this fucking desk over if you don't get out right now!" Indian boy quickly left the office and closed the door behind him. Donald smiled, obviously pleased he had gotten my attention.

"See what I have to do to get your attention baby? I've missed you. Why do you make me do these things." Donald tried to embrace me and I pushed him away.

"First the fuck of all, I thought we already had this fucking discussion. Let's get something straight. I am not a little kid; you will not page me to your office like this is high school and you are a fucking principal. I wasn't returning your calls for a reason. I DON'T FUCKING WANT YOU. Seriously dude. You're pathetic as fuck. Half the time I can't even feel your dick when we fuck. And truth be told you're a fucking broke ass bag of shit, 25 years older than me, you're a pervert. And trust if I told my daddy, that we were in here fucking? Consensual or not he'd have your job and your fucking head. So I'm a say this once and I'm not going to say it again. Leave me the fuck alone."

"Baby, what did I do?" Donald's eyes pleaded for some affection from me.

"Donald see you obviously don't get it. I fuck for two reasons, for love and for money. I certainly don't love you, and you surely don't have enough money for me to even consider fucking you again. This was supposed to be an arrangement, you didn't hold up your end of the bargain. So I'll get my degree like the rest of the whores at this school, one grade at a time."

"But Londyn, baby I love you."

"Love? Love? You don't even fucking know me, you're scared shitless of my father, as you should be. There's only one man outside of my father who ever loved me, and he's gone. So all that you're talking is bullshit, and spare it for someone else."

I grabbed a pen from his desk and pointed dangerously close to the center of his forehead. "I'm not playing when I say leave me the fuck alone. And if you can't, kill yourself because if my daddy gets wind of this you will wish you were dead." I dropped the pen back onto his desk and walked out. His secretary looked up from whatever pretend work she was looking at when I walked out. She frowned her face at me.

"Bitch, what the fuck are you looking at?"

"Well I never!" Secretary lady scoffed.

"Well I have, bitch so keep your eyes to yourself." After that fiasco I decided to blow off the rest of the day. School could wait. I had more important things to do.

Paulette

I was making my weekly visit to the Flying Monkey Bakery downtown, I salivated at the thought of one of those Blondie brownies in my mouth. Truly a better time was not to be had than me wandering around the bakery getting intertwined in the scents and sounds of this quaint shop. The Reading terminal was alive with the hustling and bustling cluster of shoppers. I'd normally go, spend a bit of time at the bakery, then head over to get myself some flowers. I remember when Donald would buy me flowers, every day. Where had the time gone? That was 10 years ago. Now I feel like we are strangers to each other. I remember the first day we met, I was a freshman at LaSalle and Donald was in graduate school. He told me my red hair was captivating. He was the most handsome man I had ever seen. His ivy green eyes and molten black hair only added to his perfectly chiseled features. He was strong, attentive, affectionate, and the best lover I had ever had. I fell in love the first time he held my hand. For me it has always been Donald. We had one miscarriage and one ectopic pregnancy both of which my petite frame was unable to rebound from. I packed on the pounds, used food as a crutch and I am no longer that tiny sexy red head that Donald fell so hard for in college. He is my everything. I will not let the likes of that little cum slut break apart the only good thing I have ever had in my life. My phone started ringing and it broke my train of thought.

"I could stay awake just to watch you sleeping.." The Aerosmith tune belted from my jacket pocket. It was Donald.

"Hello love!" I answered so excited that he called me.

"Paul, look I've tried. I can't do this anymore."

"Honey, do what? Please don't do this right now." A tremble began to rise in my voice. Fear grew in the pit of my stomach, what was he going to say?

"I'm sorry Paulette, really I am. Sorry that I am not the man I promised you I was going to be, that we can't have children because of my infidelity, that I sold you a dream we couldn't afford. I just can't do this, with you or with anyone."

"Donald! Donald! Don't you hang up! What the hell are you talking about? Do you want a divorce? Donald! Hello? Hello?" I looked at the phone; there was no one on the line. A few onlookers whispered as I searched around frantically for the exit sign. I ran out of Reading terminal as fast as my basketball shaped legs would carry me. My heart was racing, I prayed to the heavens that I didn't have a panic attack on my way to the school. I had to get to my husband.

Londyn

Since I was blowing off the rest of the school day, I decided to go visit Jordan's grave. I called Vincent and asked him if he would come with me. He was slowly becoming one of my favorite people. We talked all day and night, I was surely open and the most surprising thing is that he wouldn't fuck me. He met me at my car and I let him drive, I was so not up for it. Cussing Donald out had me all worked up, I needed a stiff shot of Absolut and a hard dick. If this day was going to get any better I had to have both. Vincent wrapped his arms around me and lifted me up off the ground a little. In his arms I melted. The energy he gave me always made me feel like the only woman in the world.

"Crikey I think I missed you today." Vincent's smile seemed to glow in the sun. He ran his fingers through my hair and ran his hand down the side of my face. Matter of fact, I miss you every day. Where are we going love?"

" I miss you too! I have someone I want you to meet." I instructed him through the city to the cemetery. The reds and oranges on the oak tree leaves crowned Jordan and his father's headstones gracefully. We parked at the bottom of the hill. The rustling fall breeze welcomed us.

"Darling why are we here?" Vincent searched for answers in my eyes.

"We are here to visit one of the only men who ever loved me. My last boyfriend, Jordan was murdered by someone else I love, just a little over seven months ago." A tear broke free, raced down my cheek, and collected at the inset of my collar bone.

"Are you sure you want me to be here?"

"Yes, I think I'm sure." I grabbed his hand and led my new love to meet my first love. He held me and I wept. I cried into him every touching moment I ever had with Jordan, all the pain of the past few months, the sleepless nights, the bad dreams, the other men, all the other men, and disgust I had with my father over taking from me the first man who loved me with everything he had.

"Darling I'm here and I'm not going anywhere. Though it has only been a few weeks, I don't ever want to leave. I want to stay here. I'll be here at least until January, but I want you to be my wife by then." We walked hand in hand back to the car. He opened my door, I reached over and opened his.

"Your wife?" In total shock of what he was saying, I tried my best to bore a hole through my passenger side window.

"Can we go to your place?" He placed his hand on my thigh and traveled his fingers lightly from my knee to the crease where my hip and leg connect.

"He wants to fuck! Finally!" My pussy danced at the thought of his tongue playing inside me. I had him pull over so I could drive. I sped over the expressway like my ass was on fire. I hadn't fucked anyone since Trevor and that was at least over a month ago. Poor Miss Kitty needed a good beating. We always pulled into the estate the back way so daddy wouldn't see Vincent in the car. He marveled at the scenery and landscaping. He had never seen the house during the day time. He had a look on his face like he had never seen a mansion in person. It was similar to the look Jordan had the first time I snuck him into the pool house. Once inside the door Vincent snatched my shorts and they fell to my ankles. Before I could step out of them he scooped me up and pinned me to the wall, just above his shoulders. His mouth met with my panties and shortly his tongue searched for the button that would turn me from 0 to 60 in 2.5 licks. He carried me up the stairs and laid me across my plush purple comforter. He stared at me with his ocean blue eyes, searching for something I wasn't sure I had within me. He began tracing my body with his fingertips slowly kissing each spot he touched.

"You know what I love about Londyn?" He kissed my lips softly. "I love Londyn's eyes, her lips, her hands..." as he spoke each word in that twisted Aussie drawl he kissed each of those points on my body, his accent made every word sound heavenly. The heat from my body radiated off me. I wanted so bad for him to take me. My pussy was pulsating with so much force I was sure he could feel it. He started kissing the inside of my thighs and slowly made his way back to that spot. He kissed it softly, whispering quietly into it sent vibrations up through my hips. As his obvious oral fixation became nearly unbearable my thighs tightened around his head. He paused briefly and looked up from his meal.

"Trust me darling." And I did, my legs fell back open and he dove back in. I nearly blacked out as an orgasm washed over me and I was unable to control myself. Eyes closed I reached for his perfectly spiked blonde hair and ran my neatly manicured nails through it. I pulled at his ears. They were perfect, he was perfect. How could it be I was falling in love with this man from half way across the world? What would I do when he left? Eyes still tightly shut I felt him make his way up to my lips. I locked my knees in hesitation, wondering if he was going to use protection. He read my mind.

"Trust me." He whispered into my ear. His bronzed skin tone meshed perfectly with my honey complexion. I held my breath as he guided himself inside of me. I winced as I allowed him to fill me up.

"I love you, Londyn. I just want to be here for you and make you happy." Vincent pulled out and re-entered me quickly. I adjusted my hips and began to rock at the same speed as him. He stopped, placed his hands on my hips and looked me in my eyes.

"Let me do this darling. I want you to enjoy me. Let me do all of the work."

"Baby, I want you to enjoy this as well."

"Look, I said don't move." The forcefulness in his tone commanded me to obey. I saw a flash of real anger in his eyes but I blinked and it was gone. Vincent put in serious work as he pumped and flexed and rode my pussy beyond its limits; he smacked, bit, and fucked places I had never known existed before today. I felt another orgasm rolling up in me from the bottom of my feet to the top of my head. I grabbed my pillow and tossed it across the room, Vincent grabbed my hands and pinned them down.

"Give it to me darling. It's mine, I want it."

"Oh my God, what are you fucking doing to me, Vincent I'm cum- I'm cum- I'm cumming!" I let out an earth shattering shriek and my pussy walls creamed with pleasure.

"I already came, beautiful." He kissed me on my forehead and went to shower. I passed out.

***

It was nearly dusk when I came to after being fucked thoroughly to sleep. My eyelids parted slowly, searching the now dark corners of my room for Vincent's silhouette. Nothing. I checked the bathroom, downstairs in the living room, the kitchen, the deck, and the pool. Still nothing. A little upset that he would leave without letting me know, I went back upstairs and sunk into the spot in my memory-foam mattress where he had laid hours before. I grabbed my phone hoping to have something from him that would say why he left. That's exactly what there was, one lone text message from Vincent made up for his disappearing act.

Hello Darling, had to leave and you looked so beautiful laying there I didn't want to wake you. Talk to you soon.

I had butterflies in my stomach. I couldn't wait till the next time I got to see Vincent. My Vincent.

Chapter 21

Donald

In the grand scheme of things, I felt as though I was actually doing Paulette a favor. Rather than feign this marriage any longer, I was going to end it. Since our vows touted till death do us part, I was going to hold up my end of the bargain. Seven shots of whiskey in, I pulled out the giant bottle of Ibuprofen I kept in my desk drawer for days when the knee I injured playing football acted up. I juggled a handful and took them back with another double shot. "Who would have ever thought my life would have amounted to this." I was talking just to hear the sound of my own voice. My grandmother always said you weren't crazy if you talked to yourself, only if you answered yourself. "I have lived my life with as much class and valor as humanly possible." I took another shot of whiskey from my coffee cup. "God Dammit Londyn, what the hell was I getting myself into with you? Why don't you want to work things out? I would leave Paulette, in a New York minute, just to be able to have my way with your pretty little ass. I knew you were trouble the moment I laid eyes on you. Daughter of the most high powered attorney in the tri-state area, young, beautiful and willing to fuck. Just the way I like them." I pushed away from my desk and grabbed another handful of pills, chucking those back as well.

"Londyn, I would have given you everything, you could have had everything." I stumbled over to the window, and gazed at all of the students shuffling their way to class and through life. "If you idiots only knew that college won't fucking help you, four years of college at Ivy League, a master's, numerous certifications and look where I am! Nowhere. Lonely and ending it all because I'm too scared to tell my wife that I'm in love with another woman; a woman who doesn't want me." More pills, more whiskey. The room was spinning at rapid speed and I wasn't sure if it was the whiskey or the pills. The last thing I heard was Paulette's voice as she burst through the door. "DONALD!"

Paulette

I burst through the door of Donald's office panicked and afraid. Unsure of what he had done to himself I screamed his name. Rushing to his side I checked his pulse while his secretary called 911. I kissed his lips, he was out cold, and sweating. I plopped onto the floor and held his head in my lap, the students in the waiting area were trying to peak into his office to see exactly what was going on.

"Get away from here or I'll have you expelled!" I bellowed. My tears stained the collar of his dress shirt. I wept for him, for the children we should have had, for the love we had at one time but now seemed to be as distant as strangers. I rocked him back and forth and prayed to whatever gods were listening. As we awaited the paramedics my mind raced, this was her fault.

She drove him to do this to himself. His life hung in the balance and I was about to clip the rope at the end of hers. More than ever now, I realized, Londyn had to go. The ambulance finally arrived and the medics intubated him, my heart broke as he was strapped to the gurney for transport. His chest bucked and he began to seize as they attempted to wheel him out of his office. I couldn't take it anymore. Once he was in the ambulance I got into my car to follow them over. I texted the drycleaner.

Me: Are the plans in place? She has to go. He replied simply.

Drycleaner: Yes, meet me on the pier tomorrow by the time you get there it will already be done.

***

I popped three Ativan as I paced back and forth in the emergency room. A beautiful African-American woman, came out to discuss what was going on with Donald.

"Mrs. Jones? I'm Dr. Stern." Her voice was sweet like she'd never gone through a day of pain in her life. I noticed the stunning diamond on her ring finger. *"Just married,"* I thought to myself.

"I am she." My nerves were rattling me to my core. My hand shook terribly as she reached out for it.

"I'm sorry to say Mrs. Jones but we have your husband in a medically induced coma right now. The lethal dose of pain pills and alcohol should have killed him. While it did not take his life it did cause him to have a series of terrible seizures, and a mild stroke which we have to have him sedated while we figure out our options from this point."

I began to cry uncontrollably. How could Donald do this to us? What am I going to do without him? "Am I able to go see him?"

"Yes you may, but please be quick about it."

I walked back to the ICU side of the emergency room and covered my mouth in shock when I got to where he was. Taped up, blood vessels in his face burst from the seizure, hands pinned to his sides, tubes everywhere. I ran my fingers through his hair, waiting and hoping to get a response from him. Something to let me know he was in there. Nothing at all, not even a twitch. I needed to be a better wife to him, had I done so he wouldn't be in the hospital right now in limbo between life and death. How did our white picket fence life turn so cold and gray in a matter of a few months. *"I can't wait for this little bitch to be dead so we can move on."* I just want my life back. More than anything, I want my husband back.

Chapter 22

Londyn

My side ached as I rolled over to grab my phone which had been ringing non-stop since before the sun came up. "What the hell does Allen want this early, damn!" I started not to answer but as good as I felt that I was in after yesterday's sex-capade there was nothing that Allen or anyone else could say to spoil my mood.

"What Allen?" I murmured into the phone.

"Good morning, my precocious princess. I pray all is well with you this morning my queen. Might I enjoy the first meal of the day with you?"

"Allen, I haven't talked to you in three weeks really since you pulled that bullshit at Fogo De Chao on my birthday. Now you are calling me like nothing was wrong. Vincent and I are together, you're going to have to accept that."

"Londyn, please this man is a killer. He is not who he says he is, I did my research he's not even from Australia!"

"Allen please, you are delusional, it's really too early for this shit. Miss me with the bullshit. If you are going to call and talk bad about my man I don't want to talk."

"Goddess, my apologies I won't disturb you any longer." I hung up on him, and turned back over to grab some more z's before I got up and soaked my poor pussy. Maybe later I'll call Vincent and see if he wanted to come punish Miss Kitty some more.

Giuseppe

Early in the morning is when I get to do the majority of my thinking. I was at my desk looking over briefs for an upcoming case when my phone rang.

"Giuseppe Taliaferro speaking," I cleared my voice and took a sip of the piping hot coffee Rosie had brought for me just a few moments before.

"Ay, Mr. G, its Demetrius Aramoso. I have some information for you. I owe you one so I wanted to give you a heads up."

"Proceed." Tension formed at the base of my neck unsure of what this little fuck up had to say that would be of any value to me.

"Your daughter Londyn, has she stepped on anyone's toes or pissed anyone off lately?" His voice was shakey at best, as if he could be eradicated for the information he was about to give me.

"Not that I know of Demetrius, what is going on, let's cut through the bullshit."

He exhaled deeply. "I received information from a very credible source that a contract has been placed on your daughter's head. $100k for her death, she's been sleeping with the husbands of some women who play for keeps. And the fella they hired goes by the name The Drycleaner. He is 75-0, he never misses. I thought ya should know, Mr. G so you could do something."

"I have to go, thank you." I slammed the phone down into its cradle. What the hell had Londyn gotten herself into now? If a hundred thousand dollar contract had been placed and paid there was nothing I could do to stop it just short of banning her from leaving the house. I stormed out into the hallway where Thomas was seated near the front door.

"Basement, now," I flung the basement door open and descended the steps three at a time. Behind the personal bar I had built in the basement I popped the cork on the bottle of tequila my father bought the day Londyn was born. Aged 22 years, now was as good a time as any. I turned the bottle up to my lips and swallowed as much as my throat could bear. I fought back the urge to cry. At this point a plan escaped me, I can'tbelieve someone is trying to kill my daughter, my baby girl.

Thomas bounded down the steps unsure of what was going on.

"Sir, what's the problem?" His Irish accent shone through the most when he was upset or worried.

"It's Londyn, this stupid kid, my stupid kid. She's gone and fucked someone's husband. Now information just came to me that there was a one hundred thousand dollar contract placed on her head. They've hired someone called the dry cleaner. Do you know anything about him?"

"The dry cleaner? He's a fella out of Jersey, really good at what he does apparently. Never misses." The words "never misses" sunk into the pit of my stomach like an anvil. I had to do something.

"I should confine her to the house to see if I can get my hands on this drycleaner and either pay him off or make him disappear."

"That's your only option, if she needs to leave she's going to have full security detail and the car service, but even that may not stop him sir."

"She's not going to need to leave; I will have her school work brought home. She will be pissed, but I would rather have her alive and pissed off, than, than..." I couldn't say the word dead. What type of parent am I? She would have been better off with Rebecca at least then she would have been alive. What would Rebecca think of me, she entrusted me to take care of her daughter, and I failed. Did I protect her too much? Not enough?

I should have told her about Sergio and Jordan, I was planning on it just not yet. I wanted to take her away on a vacation, to try and reconnect. Lately it seems like it's been all about money with her, or work with me. I took another gulp of the tequila. Thomas couldn't mask the concern in his eyes. I sparked up a stogie and started to pace the floor behind the bar.

"There has to be a solution, something that won't piss her off to the high heavens."

"Sir, you are already on her bad side, there's nothing that you can do or say that isn't going to piss her off." Thomas poured himself a shot of tequila, he was as much a part of this family as anyone and we were amid a crisis at this very moment.

"I'm going back to my office; I need to talk to her right now." I climbed the stairs back to my office, uncertain how the next few moments were going to pan out.

Londyn

My father paged me through the intercom system with so much anger in his voice I thought for sure I had landed on page six again. I rushed through the house, nearly killing myself, sliding across Rosie's freshly mopped kitchen floor. Once inside his office the energy was heavy. I could tell he needed to tell me something but I wasn't quite sure what it was.

"Sit down Bella." His voice was eerily calm, normally when upset with he would have it written all over his face. But he looked very stoic.

"What's up daddy?" I folded my legs up behind me and took a seat in the chair to the right of his desk.

"There is something going on, I'm not sure why. There was a contract placed on your head and until I find out who was hired to do the job I need you to stay in the house. Under 24 hour surveillance where I can keep my eyes and ears on you at all times."

"Why the hell would anyone want to kill me?"

"Sleep with anyone's husband lately?" The snide tone in my father's voice stung. He knew all about my little affairs.

"Daddy, I have school. I'm doing well, what am I supposed to do?" I rolled my eyes and let the frustration in my tone speak for me.

"First of all Donald's in the hospital, so I don't have any other direct contacts at the school to keep you safe. I will arrange for your teachers to give your work to that boy; what's his name? The dread head."

"Allen? Daddy, I'm not even speaking to him right now, between you and him, you are both some weirdos. He came up to me and Vincent a few weeks ago shouting something out about him being an assassin or something. You guys are crazy."

"I forbid you to leave this house... until this is figured out."

My pocket vibrated. I grabbed my phone to check my message. It was from Vincent. It was simple. He said:

Darling I need to c u again.

My father was fuming now. I smiled at my phone, and texted a reply.

Daddy is tripping. B there soon. Can't wait for round 2!

"Daddy, I've gotta go, I don't have time for this. I'm grown and you aren't going to confine me in the house. I'm not scared of anything that anyone can do to me."

I got up and ran out of his office. I quickly zipped past the guards. Just as I went to open the front door my father grabbed my hand.

"Londyn please. Out there I can't protect you." His eyes pleaded for me to listen. But Vincent wanted to see me and my pussy was wet and needed him. After that day in the pool house I couldn't wait for him to fill me up again.

"Daddy I'm a big girl. I can manage to go visit my friend without getting killed!" I snatched my hand away from him and jumped into my car. I could see my father getting into his car in my rearview. I floored the gas as I sped out of the drive way. I wanted to get to Vincent as fast as possible. As I flew down the road that led to our estate and past the first freeway exit. I figured that my father would grab the first exit and I could lose him by taking the second one. Close on my tail I turned the bend onto St. Mary's Drive, I pressed my brake to slow down, nothing. I panicked and tried to fucking put my foot through the ground, pressing the brake so hard. My car went into a tailspin. I closed my eyes. The car did a complete 180° spin and was barreling at full speed towards the only other car on the road- my father's. My mind raced, my heart nearly beat out of my chest. I wanted to cry but fear kept the tears at bay. A flash of my father teaching me how to drive came across my mind, then, tea with my grandmother; s'mores with Rosie; gardening with Thomas; Jordan's arms wrapped around me; my first kiss with Vincent. My father, the first man who ever loved me. Everything went black as the sound of crushing metal and breaking glass were the only audible noises. Not even the sound of my own breath could be heard.

Giuseppe

I raced after Londyn as quickly as I could. She has her mother's stubborn temper; she does exactly the opposite of what she is told.

"Always the bullshit with you, Londyn." I took a swig of brandy from the flask in the center console of my car. The slight sting to my chest gave me the momentum I needed to get into this high speed car chase with my daughter. My pride and joy, my daughter. There was a time when Londyn wouldn't have dared to make a move without first requesting permission from me. She's always been a free spirit, but when it came to me she was always in accordance. I don't know where I went wrong. Here I am, 42 years old, racing down the road at 90 miles per hour after my daughter, on the same road I drove bringing her home from the hospital. I saw her skip the first freeway exit and go up around the bend. I sped up to catch up to her. What I saw next was unexplainable. I watched my daughter's car, my only child, my baby's car spiraling out of control and heading straight towards me. I cut my wheel to the right and fastened my seatbelt. I knew what was coming, but if she hit the side of my car, then the chances of her surviving would be higher than if I would have allowed it to be a head on collision. I took another swig of brandy, kissed the cross that hung around my neck. As I braced myself for impact I made a deal with God.

"Spare her life God, portami signore. Ive fatto molte cose cattive. Ricambio Londyn's vita[6]."

As the impact of my daughter's car reverberated through my body, my eyes closed. *"Thank you."*

Paulette

The sky was overcast when I got to the pier. I clutched my purse closely to me and shoved my now ringless left hand into the pocket of my windbreaker. The walk to the end of the pier was extensive; each step brought the realization of what I had done. I was long past the point of no return. I thought I would at least have Donald, but his own guilty conscience wouldn't allow him to face the humiliation of a public scrutiny, so there he lay in a coma, hanging in limbo between life and death. My pace quickened, I just wanted to get this over with. I looked up and nearly waddled right into his back. Not at all like I imagined him, beautiful in stature with the most amazing bronze tan I've seen since Donald and I went to Bermuda. *"Dammit Donald. I can't go five minutes without something reminding me of you, of us."* I blinked back my tears and tapped

---

[6]Take me lord. I've done many bad things. Spare Londyn's life

155

the gentleman towering over me as close to his shoulder as my dumpy upper extremities would allow me to.

"Drycleaner?" I looked up into his aqua baby blues and was hard pressed to believe these were the eyes of a killer.

"Hey, enough with the drycleaner shit, just call me V. I take it you have the rest of my money, because the job was done. I sent her an urgent text message to meet me. The rest is history, ya know?" His voice was not at all like the foreign accent I had heard in our earlier conversations.

"How are you certain that she will die?"

"I never miss, check this out." V flexed his well-toned biceps and I felt warmness between my legs. *"How am I getting excited during this morbid situation?"* He whipped out a small tablet notebook and flipped through a few pages on the internet browser. He handed it to me and folded his arms. The smug grin across his face depicted he was quite pleased with himself. My hand began to shake and I nearly dropped the tablet.

"Ay, watch it, I just got that!"

My trembling hand met my mouth in utter disbelief. The scrolling news feed on Channel 5 News website read: Just In: Taliaferro pronounced dead at scene of grisly car accident.

More news at 11.

I handed him back his little device and reached into my purse to hand him the remaining payment. He quickly snatched the travelers cheques from me and folded them precisely, placing them into a hidden compartment in the seam of his cargo shorts.

"Pleasure doing business with you lady. If I never see you again it will be too soon…G'day mate."

I stood feet firmly planted unable to move as I watched V jump down onto the steps next to the pier, and in one fail swoop position himself onto a jet ski and make a bee line for the sunset. Somehow I thought that getting her out of our lives would give me a whole, complete feeling. All I feel at this point is empty loneliness. The little girl from Stamford, Connecticut, turned to murder for hire to hold on to the remnants of a marriage built on fallacies from its inception.

The clamoring of my cell phone brought me back to reality. It was Ericka.

"Hello?"

"Hay, boo. You see the news? Let's go celebrate with martinis!"

"I could use a stiff one right now, I'll be there shortly I was at the office." Lies came so easily to me now. The drive back to the country club would prove to be the longest Id' ever taken; alone.

Thomas

The dull murmur of the pulse ox machine was the only thing I could hear. I sat at her bedside unable to move from my post. It had been 2 days. *"She simply must be ok. She has to be ok."* Every so often she would stir softly in her sleep. She had been out cold since the accident, I wasn't quite sure how to tell her about all that had transpired. Members of the staff stood guard, and the three heads of the other families sat in the waiting room patiently awaiting the news that the only heir to the Taliaferro empire was going to make it. Nightfall swept over the hospital quickly and I was about to step outside to grab a few puffs of my cigar when she moved. A faint moan escaped her lips. The anguish was evident in her face but I touched her arm and she responded. Battered and bruised she was alive none-the-less.

Her normally honey skin tone was ashen. Her hair matted and the traction she was in, I'm sure for her, was unbearable. I grabbed a few fingers on her now casted arm and kissed them lovingly. Her eyes parted slowly. She looked to me, and then around the room scanning back and forth three or four times obviously looking for her father. All of the staff members had their heads down. No one wanted it to be their eyes that let Londyn know the truth.

"Thomas?" Londyn managed to sputter out between her swollen lips. I contemplated my answer. What should I say? How will I tell her this? "You guys leave us alone a moment."

"Good Evening, Don Londyn"

I watched in sheer and utter horror as Londyn's eyes widened. Her greatest fear had been realized.

"MY FATHER IS GONE?"

The End

FEAR ME
RESPECT IS OVERRATED

LONDYN
RISE OF A FEMALE DON

a novel by
SANKOFA

Well it's been a while but I'm back with a vengeance, between running an empire and raising my baby son, I've had to grow up faster than I ever anticipated. I made my list, and checked it twice, if you're on it, then I'm sorry, your number is up, starting with the bitches who put a contract out on my head. I am Londyn, and this is a story of murder, mayhem and revenge.

This is the rise of a female don.

Preface: Book 2 Rise of a Female Don

The cathedral at 10th and Arch was filled to the brim with people mourning the death of the late great Giuseppe Taliaferro. Drones of people filed in a few at a time to walk past his casket. I sat in the front row, next to Thomas unwilling to let go of his hand. My wide brimmed hat and Jackie O style glasses hid from the world my blood shot eyes. But my broken heart was on my sleeve for the whole church to see. Casted foot and wrist made it nearly impossible to stand for a long period of time. Once everyone had come in to pay their respects Thomas and I walked up to my father's coffin for the last time. As I stood in front of the most handsome man I had ever known I felt a hand on my back. My head shot around and I nearly fell over. I was looking at a woman whose face was the same as mine.

"I'm so sorry for your loss Londyn Marie."

"Who the fuck are you?" I had just gotten out of the hospital it had only been a week, I was still on pain meds so I wasn't quite sure what I was seeing. I looked at Thomas, he seemed to know her. "Fuck this shit, I'm outta here."

I steadied myself on my crutches and made a b-line for the side exit as fast as those crutches would carry me. Once outside in the courtyard I prayed rain would come so I wouldn't have to face the harsh reality that was about to hit me like a ton of bricks. Thomas came outside after me.

"Miss Londyn please we must go back inside. They won't start the funeral without you."

"Well, let them wait, who the fuck is that woman with my face Thomas? Hunh? How do you know who she is?"

The woman emerged from the same door of the church I had come out of, she was beautiful, the same honey tone as me, her eyes the same as mine, nose... identical.

"Thomas why didn't you tell me my father had another child? What the fuck?" Thomas looked confused, searching for the appropriate words to say during this awkward moment.

"Bitch look, let me tell you something you may be my sister, but my father left all the money to me, so please don't think your broke ass is going to be coming to me for one damn dime. I don't believe in charity."

"Londyn, I am your mother." My world spun, so it took for my father to die for my mother to come out of hiding where ever she had been at for 22 years.

"Bitch please I don't have a mom."

Rise of a Female Don- Coming Spring 2013

PENNSYLVANIA

The **MAN·U·L**

Rules to life by Farrah Monroe Evans (F. Me)

C.M SPENCE

My mom knew I'd be a stone cold freak. She named me after two bombshells, taught me how to use what I have to get what I want and then died when I was twelve, leaving me to fend for myself. Truth is, I was on my own long before my mom died. She was so busy trying to find love that she couldn't spare time to give me any. So I found it in odd forms.

The grief counselor that was assigned to me after my mom died really seemed to care about me. So I pretended to be consumed with grief to keep going back. The in-school suspension monitor was a pervert and would let me leave early in exchange for a peek down my shirt. So I spent most of my ninth grade year with his eyes between my breasts. And the first guy I ever loved had a girlfriend when I met him. He said he was torn between me and her. He loved us for different reasons. But, he could only love her publicly. So I accepted my role as a side chick.

That was many moons and men ago. And although my first encounter as a side chick was thrust upon me, it was one of the best things that ever happened in my life. I got older and wiser with time and vowed only to be "the other woman."

I'm Farrah Monroe Evans. Better known as. F.Me.... I'm straight to the point. I like sex and lots of it. But I only have sex with unavailable men. Married. Engaged. Or otherwise involved. And the more "involved" a man is, the more thunderous my orgasm.

I had just had one all over the face of my current beau. He had spent all morning texting me about his wife and how he was falling back in love with her. He spent the last twenty minutes getting his upper lip glazed. There was something about the way he talked about her that turned me on. His honest desire to be faithful to her made me want him more. Knowing that the fingers that were just gripping my thighs would soon be interlaced with hers while talking about their future drove me wild. And she had no idea that future included me. The only thing that made the sight of his fingers better was the fact that he was wearing a wedding band. The thought alone made me shove his head back between my legs.

I know...I'm fucked up. And the men that I love never understand. But, they never say no either. Never. I could get them to get out of their bed at 4 am to come see me if I wanted to. I would never do that, though. Never.

This is a dangerous game I play. There are rules. The risk is high. The reward is priceless. And I always score. I explain the terms to my men. And though they think I'm bullshitting, they agree. To make sure, I write my initials on a piece of paper and make them read it aloud.

"F. Me?" They always say it with uncertainty in their voice.

"I'd be happy to," I always reply.

And from there it begins. A full blown relationship that can never leave the confines of my apartment. No dates. No holidays. Just stolen moments, sheet ripping sex, and his commitment to someone else.

My rules are simple.

1) Never spend money on me.
2) Never take your wedding ring off around me.
3) Never question my loyalty.

My men love rule #1. The men I love aren't rich. They rarely have any extra funds to spend without their wives noticing, anyway. I don't fuck for money. I go to work every day and I pay my own bills. I only require that they bring their A game the first time we sleep together. Every time after that, they want to bring their A game to keep up with me. Them falling in love is just an added bonus.

Rule #2 causes some problems sometimes. Men who cheat are used to having to lie. They can slip their wedding ring off in the blink of an eye if they think it will serve as a barrier to getting some new pussy. But, a wedding ring opens my legs wider than a hillbilly's toothless grin at a ho down. My men are disturbed by that at first, though. The presence of the band is a constant reminder of her. Of the vows he took that he breaks more with each deep, long thrust inside me. That's his problem. Not mine.

Which leads me to Rule #3. I refuse to date more than one unavailable man at a time. When I'm with someone, I'm with them only. They get all my attention. They get all my love. No matter how sick and twisted it is. Without fail, I get accused of cheating every single time I start a relationship. Common sense would tell you that any woman who requires her man to have another woman would naturally have another man of her own. But there's nothing common about how I love them and it doesn't make much sense to anyone but me. Their inability to be faithful has nothing to do with my desire to love hard.

This is an isolating existence. I can't gush to my friends about romantic dates. There are none. I can't vent about arguments with my man. They would say I have no business arguing with them in the first place. So I strategically create pseudo-relationships with out of town men who don't exist. Or I work two jobs all year round to say I'm too busy to date.

I made the mistake of telling a friend about my weakness for wedded men. At first she disagreed but said it was my life to live or lose as I pleased. Then she found out she was the other woman. So she gave it a go. She told her borrowed boy toy that she knew he was cheating on her but if he could keep both her and his main chick satisfied, she was okay. And they proceeded…Until one day her jealous ass broke into the home he shared with said main chick, armed with pictures and text messages and emails to prove how much he loved her. She walked in to the sounds of him banging his girl's back out asking her to marry him. Personally, I would have came all over their carpet. Instead, she flew into a rage, caught a breaking and entering charge and received an all-expenses paid trip to county lock up. Most chicks just ain't built for this.

Correction…most chicks aren't built for the acceptance of this. I don't know one woman who hasn't been cheated on. And of those women, each of them lived to tell about it. They moved on and dated someone else. Some of them found Mr. Right. Some of them are still looking. But, each of them went through emotional exercises that gave their hearts and my ears a workout. *Is he lying like so-and-so? What does he really mean when he says he loves me? My ex used to wear boxer briefs and so does he. That's proof he's a cheater!*

I get to skip all of that. The bullshit that women wonder about, I know up front. Whether you find out about it from the door or by having the other woman standing on your doorstep, it doesn't change the fact that chances are…the man you love probably also loves someone else.

And that doesn't negate the fact that he loves you. Aaron Taylor loved me in eleventh grade. And he loved Unique Montgomery at the same time. She was shy and sheltered. She didn't like to hang out much and didn't know a whole lot. Although, I didn't know nearly as much as I thought I did at 16, I was popular, outgoing, the head of my class and expected to be the mayor of our small town. But it was well known that my overprotective uncle who stepped in to care for me after my mom passed would die himself before he allowed me to date. It was easier for me to fill my calendar with extracurricular activities than think about my empty list of suitors. I was perfect for Aaron. Someone who wanted nothing more than to have someone to love but couldn't do it in front of anyone.

When I went off to college, my busy schedule continued. I kept my nose stuck so far in my textbooks trying to keep my scholarship, I left no room for any guys to have it open. I wasn't blind, though. I was attracted to a few guys while I was there. One was on the football team. One was in my chemistry classes. One was always stepping and party walking with his pretty boy fraternity brothers. And they all had girlfriends.

My infatuation with unavailable men started long before my college days. Or before Aaron Taylor, for that matter. Ironically, it started with my mother. I watched her love my dad for as long as I could remember. There was nothing she wouldn't do for him. And when they looked at each other, the love they between them was undeniable. I wanted that kind of love. Lucky for me, I got it. My dad had been married for 20 years before he met my mom. Them falling in love never changed his marital status. Nor did it stop him from going home to his wife every night. That was a minor detail.

It was just after 1:30 in the afternoon on a Friday. Warren Logan met me for our weekly lunch date. He had rearranged his schedule as a Coca Cola deliveryman to be able to see me. We had been dating for eight months and I was falling for him more with each passing week. I met him when he made a delivery at the pharmacy I work at. At first I paid him no attention. He came in all the time. We exchanged pleasantries but nothing more. Then I noticed a different delivery man came in his place two weeks in a row. When he returned, I joked that I thought he had been fired. He stated he was away on his honeymoon and brandished his new ring. I was immediately interested.

"What are you thinking about?" I hadn't even noticed that he stopped eating me out.

"Huh," I asked blankly.

"What are you thinking about," he asked slowly. He wiped his face.

"How much I love you."

He kissed me instead of verbally responding. That was all the answer I needed. I wrapped my legs around his back and pushed his hips into mine. I braced myself and waited for him to slip inside me like I knew he would. His force still caught me off guard and made me gasp. I knew him so well.

He squeezed himself inside me and filled my already contracting pussy like my hips in too tight pants from last summer. I involuntarily moaned. He growled. My moan always turned him on. He said that alone could make him cum.

"I missed you so much," I whispered into his neck.

"I missed you too," he whimpered.

I rocked my hips to meet his pace and he pounded the living daylights out of me. My moans became screams and please for him or God to have mercy on me. Clearly it would have to be God because Warren wasn't letting up. Beads of sweat formed across his nose and his nostrils flared. I was stealthily quiet for a few seconds as he attempted to drill a hole in my midsection. I tightened myself around his dick one time and let out the longest, sexiest moan I could muster.

He ripped his pulsating penis from within me as fast as he could. I pushed him on his back and stuffed it in my mouth. He emptied his love into my throat and emptied his lungs with a scream that made me proud. That was the sound of undeniable satisfaction.

"Don't touch me," he said when I laid next to him. I giggled. "You are evil." That made me bust out laughing.

He panted and tried to catch his breath. I grabbed the frozen Gatorade I had waiting for him off my dresser. I put the dripping bottle up to his searing hot skin. He jumped like someone had stabbed him. Warren sat his head up slightly to take a drink. He gulped the contents of the bottle and crushed it in his hand to pulverize the ice. He slammed his head back down on the pillow I had given him. He was exhausted.

The sight of my man lying in my bed drained made me tingle. He wiped his face with his left hand and I saw his ring. Fire ripped through my hips and I moaned again. I immediately opened my top drawer, grabbed my bullet and pressed the silver coolness against my hot button. It only took a few seconds for my back to arch, my toes to curl, and the puddle begin to spread on the sheets.

"Are you serious?" Warren asked in a high pitched voice. "Girl, you are a nympho, for real."

"Oh hush," I playfully scolded him. "Get _____ both of us to head back to work. You go _____ money for your pretty, little wife."

I walked out the room before he could re_____ comment. I knew it would piss him off b_____ care. I know his marriage requirement is my rule but I can't help bt to get jealous sometimes. My venom filled sarcasm was an unfortunate consequence of him dealing with me. It was a small price to pay for good pussy on the side.

A Novel By

Lynn J

Amanda Keating Must Die – A teen novel from the mind of Lynn Jones

Amanda Keating is you know, THAT GIRL, the captain of the Cheer Squad, class president, leader of the future teachers of tomorrow, and Joel Millers girlfriend. You know that kind of girl who barfs rainbows and

Introducing the Mean Girl Murders

A Novel By

Lynn Jones

pisses sunshine. Everybody hates her she's so freaking perfect. Like how are you 17 and you've never had a pimple? I share she's a cyborg. That's beside the point, she can have anyone and anything she wanted, but she just had to have what was mine, and that's when I decided, that little Miss Unicorns and Cupcakes Amanda Keating; had to DIE.

Interrogation

The chair in the investigation room was cold, donning just my pajama pants and my coat I sat in this room in the Charlesdale police station, pissed off. Charlesdale is one of those towns where everyone knows everyone. The chief of police is married to my Aunt Rachel, the butcher Mr. Pablo is my dad's best friend and there is only one doctor's office, Dr.Kelson. In order to get any kind of action, or fun we have to travel 45 minutes into Boston. But I like it for the most part.

My name is Alexia King, im 15 and im sitting in the police station being investigated for the murder of the most hated girl in the entire world. The super bitch as I like to normally refer to her just happens to have my same initials. Amanda and I use to be best friends up until she betrayed me.

When I say best friends I mean from when we were too little to realize what best friends were. We did everything together, until she changed.

Dad looked at me like I had stolen his puppy as I turned my mood ring back and forth. He shook his head continually back and forth. I was quite annoyed to be sitting there having to explain to them why I had killed Amanda Who cares she's gone I had done the world a favor. The United States of America should give me a medal for ridding the world of her! I laughed to myself thinking about it.

Detective Gheret came in and looked at me like he was disgusted. He had the kind of belly that hung down over his belt. Aa butt gutt is what we call it! Old boy had deffinently had one to many visits to the donut shop.

Slamming the stack of evidence mounted against me onto the steel table Detective Gheret took his seat in front of me. His key clanged against the metal chair which looked like it was going to fold in at any moment.

"So Alexia," Detective donut, I mean Detective Gheret said peering out from behind his round cheeks and small glasses. " tell me what happened."

"Well if you really want to know what happened I have to start at the beginning ."

"The beginning?"

"Yea, the 9th grade!"

The look on his face was one of exhaustion. Im sure he was certain it was going to be a very long night.

AK + AK

BFF 4E

Highschool

Is gonna be

Chapter 1 – Cheerleading Tryouts

The sun was crazy hot on the first day of cheerleading try outs. Since the 7th grade we had plotted and planned for this day. Now here we were 8th graders ready to go to high school for the first time next school year trying with all our might to make the cheer squad.

Tryouts for the CSH Bearcats Varsity Squad was a huge deal. They were only the best squad around for at least 100 miles. They took states every year easily. The football team was just as good. Especially with the amazing Joel Ethan Miller as their quarter back and star player. He is something like a phenomenon and he just so happens to be the love of my life. Yes I love Joel, he's awesome. Anyway, he had been starting varsity qb since 9th grade which is unheard of around these parts. Last season he ran for over 137 yards passing, was all conference and as a junior has major scouts offering him scholarships already. But back to what I was saying. It was the first day of tryouts. Amanda and I were both so nervous.

Dressed in matching hot pink Nike tanks and biker shorts we surely looked the part. Her jet black hair was neatly cupped into the perfect bun as we stretched in the Saturday afternoon sun.

Amandas eyes glistened like freshly printed money everytime she looked my way. We each tucked out matching AK necklaces into our tank tops as Coach Blount bellowed through her bull horn.

"3 minutes till on line, 3 minutes till online. Get it together or get left ladies!" Coach was in crazy shape, if you have ever seen those women body builders she could certainly fall in line with them easily. Her abs looked like they responded for her everytime she spoke.

"Umm Lex are you ready?" Amanda whispered.

We stood side by side prepared to cartwheel and herchy our way onto the varsity squad thus securing our positions in highschool as popular girls for our entire highschool career. The music blared and Coach Blount rapid fired moves at us. 3 seniors walked in and out of the rows of us girls marking x's next to our names.

The first round was over and my thighs were on fire. I just knew at the end of this I was going to have 3rd degree burns over most of my body. I looked to my left and Amnada had barely broken a sweat. She was rearing to go. Her skin looked radiant and every move she made was with the accuracy of a born cheerleader.

"Come on Lex! Lets do this!"

"Well aren't you all puppies and unicorn puke!" No smiling there I felt like crap.

"Whatever, don't be such a red head." Coach Blount interrupted our mini bitch fest.

"Shut up the noise ladies or take 4 laps."

I quickly took a swig of my water and prepped for the next round of physical agony. Round two was routines only. The cheer captaind showed us the routine in 3 parts and we had a few mins to learn it and perform it with nauseating precision.

As I went over the dance and fell in line I prayed the girl in front of me who was a porker didn't attempt the jump in the middle of the routine and mistakenly dislocate my jaw. Amanda was more ready then ever. I looked over to see her hands folded in solemn prayer to the cheer Gods. As we got started the cheer captains called our numbers. If your number was called that meant you didn't get to advance to the next round. As I was twisting and turning my hips to the sound of Fergie I awas giving it everything I had. I was not prepared for what I heard next.

"47, 47 step out." The blonde haired devil, I mean cheer captain bellowed into her bull horn. My heart sank . Amanda flashed me a brief look of empathy but kept going. From the bleachers I got a better look at what was taking place on the field. My gaze was fixed on number 48, Amanda. She was better than some of the cheer captains. She was amazing! Her twists and turns were pure perfection.

2 hours and several routines later, the bleachers were filled with outcasts, rejects and the others who just didn't make the cut. 6 girls remained. Of the 6 Amanda was the best of them all. Surely fatigued she showed no signs of stopping or giving in. I knew without a shadow of a doubt that Amanda was not only a newly

appointed member of the Bearcats Varsity Cheerleading squad, but also that she was going to be popular. More popular then the two of us could ever imagine.

Walking home after that grueling day I was a little down.

"Oh come on Lex, you act like this is going to change things! I'll just have to hang out with you after cheer camp. "

"Promise?"

"On everything in the world." We locked pinky's and crossed the street to walk down the hill towards our development.

A red convertible Mustang approached us really fast with a few members of the cheerleading team in it. Behind the wheel was Lindsay Andrews, even a bigger bitch then Amanda is now.

"Hey Mand," *Who even calls her Mand?* I thought to myself. "We need to go over some routines, I know its no official that your on the squad yet, but we need you to come with!"

" Umm ok, sure I guess can my friend Alexia come?"

"Who? Oh that over there?" Kelsey one of the other cheerleaders in the car. " We said you, not your shadow. Are you coming or not?"

Amanda turned to me looking for the go ahead to go on the ar ride that would in turn change the course of our friendship.

"Its cool go ahead, text me later." My mouth told her to leave but my eyes wanted her to stay. She drove off with the cheerleaders and that was the beginning of the end.

***

"So let me get this right Alexia, this is all over because she got chosen for the cheerleading squad and you didn't?" Officer Gheret looked annoyed.

I rolled my eyes cause obviously Detective Donut wasn't listening. "Aren't you hearing what im saying? Its so much deeper then just cheerleading!"

"Well please continue."

"Thank you! God I sware your dense!"

"ALEXIA Victoria King! You are in enough trouble without you being rude!"

"So like I was saying cheerleading was just the beginning but it was so much more than just that! Once school got started it all went downhill."

Dear Diary,

The first day of school totally sucked. I haven't seen Amanda in like 3 weeks and she told me things weren't going to change. Yea right! Im so over trying to keep up my end of this friendship. Since she made the varsity squad she's been so funny acting. I never imagined having to go through high school without my BFF 4E by my side. I thought about talking to her about it but she's never available. I sent her a bunch of texts and a few messages on FB, wtf!! Oh well you win some and loose some. Im hurt.

FML,

Lex <3

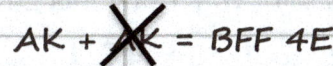

AK + ~~AK~~ = BFF 4E

Chapter 2 – No More BFF's

The hallways at CSH were a mad house, students rushing to class and pushing through and around the ones who had everything but their education on their minds. I was on day 3 of this 4 year prison sentence. I was feeling exceptionally cute in my tights, vintage flowered top and navy blue Uggs. While I wasn't the most fashionable I like what I like you know?

I hadn't seen Amanda but for a few minutes in freshman orientation and she seemed excited to see me but I could tell it was fake. I was talking to her for only like 3 minutes before her captors came and swept her away.

It was lunch time and Amanda and I ended up in line together.

"Hey Mandie. Whats new?" I almost didn't speak she was like a stranger to me. She had dyed her hair over the summer. Her jet black hair was now highlighted candy apple red in support of the school colors. "What did you do to your hair?"

"Lex!! I miss you so much. I haven't been being much of a best friend lately. I've just been super-duper busy with cheerleading and stuff." Amanda opened her cheerleading jacket and played with the charm to her necklace to kind of show me that I still meant something to her.

"I just really miss hanging out with you, I saw Joel Ethan and church Sunday and I almost died! He's so dreamy." We walked side by side to a table in the middle of the cafeteria.

"He is really cute, he's really nice too. We had to sit on the bus with the football players last weekend for the away game."

"IM DEAD! You talked to him? What did he say? How did he look? Were his teeth really straight? He smells so good. Ok Ok im rambling tell me all about it so I can write it in my Joelbook!

Amanda giggled as she popped grapes into her mouth and recounted the story word for word.

"Well I was sitting beside Declin and Adonis. Joel Ethan was behind me it was so crazy riding on a bus full of beefed up football players. They were so rowdy except Joel he just seemed to be concentrating. He and I chatted it up a little bit, he is really very nice."

"OH EM GHEE Amanda! I can't believe it! You will have to tell me in more detail when I have my Joelbook so I can write it all down!" My eyes glazed over in delight. I loved loved loved to dish about my number one boy crush in the entire world Joel Ethan Miller! We met when I was 10 and he was 13. We attend the same church and met over the summer I was going to 5th grade at vacation bible school. We often chatted while waiting for our parents to pick us up. I figured I didn't have a chance in hell with him, I was still in elementary school and he was in middle school. Then when he made varsity football in the 9th grade that dashed any hopes I had! I started a notebook dubbed "The JoelBook" the following summer and its filled to brim with things I've found out about him over the years. All his likes and dislikes. Favorite movies, and colors. I even know that he's left handed and only likes green M&M's!

He's my soulmate I just know it. As soon as I can get the opportunity to let him know he's gonna realize how so much has been missing from his life before we got together.

But anyway like I was saying I was more excited about finally getting to catch up with my bestie! We finished up lunch and walked out into the hallway together running straight into Lindsay and Kelsey and their resident flunky, Navy. Like honestly who names their kid Navy?

"Alright bff I'll catch you later!" I said to her as I headed left to go down the hallway to my first afternoon class.

"EWWW DID SHE SAY BFF? WHO STILL SAYS THAT? WHAT ARE WE IN 5TH GRADE? WHO IS SHE ANYWAY MAND?" Kelsey blurted out in the middle of the hallway. I watched as they all shared a laugh at my expense. Even Amanda who I never expected to laugh squinted her eyes and broke into a fit of laughter. Her laughs hurt most of all.

"You know what Amanda, you don't have to worry about calling me later. Or ever." There was so much venom in my words I was sure they were going to poison her like she was poisoning our friendship.

"Aww Mand, the little teeny weeny freshman said don't call her anymore. WTF? Wait wait what's your name? Alexus? Alexandria?"

"Its Alexia."

"Are you a lesbo or something why is is such a big deal that Amanda call you? What do you want to scissor her after school?" Lindsay laughed so hard she was kicking her feet up and Navy was snickering to herself, I could see in her eyes she didn't find it nearly as amusing as she pretended. I looked at Amanda for some sort of apology in her eyes. There was nothing. The eyes of my best friend were replaced with the eyes of one of them. A cyborg cheerleader/ Mean Girl. No more BFF'S.

***

"So you and Amanda stopped being friends in 9th grade, over a year and a half ago? Why kill her now?"

"Dude you really aren't listening to me. Take notes and keep up." I folded my legs into my chair. This next part was going to be the most difficult. She stole from me. She did the one thing that a real best friend would never do. For that she had to pay. In the worst way. I would never ever forgive her. They had gotten to her, transformed her into one of them. Some friend she was.

Other titles coming soon by

Sankofa

Snapped: The Man Eater

Snapped 2: Justin's Journey

Snapped 3: The HIV Murders

Snapped 4: Peach Tree Passion

Other titles coming soon by

CM Spence

Holy Trinity 2: The Prayer Circle

Grey Skies